Scoring Position

Scoring Position

A Texas Playmakers Romance

Joanne Rock

TULE
PUBLISHING

Chapter One

I T IS A truth universally acknowledged that a single woman dating in a small town will forever be matched with the exact same pool of bachelors on every matchmaking app known to womankind. Worse, if she's lived in that small town for a few years, she'll know every last one of them far too well to consider them as prospective romantic partners.

Dismally swiping left on the familiar lineup of a dozen faces in the latest app she'd tried, high school English teacher Emma Garcia sat at her desk after her students left for the weekend. Outside her classroom at Creekbend High School in Last Stand, Texas, she heard the diesel groan of buses leaving the parking lot, taking all the noise and restless excitement of her charges with them. Most of her colleagues were already pouring out the doors too, in spite of their teaching contract that said they needed to work for fifty minutes past the time of the bus departure.

How could she blame them on a Friday the week before their February break? Maybe if she had a life of her own—a family, a romantic partner—to go home to, Emma would be bolting for her compact car now too. Her one commitment was weekend dog-sitting for a friend heading out of town, but she wouldn't receive her canine guest until tomorrow morning. Now, she glanced wistfully up at the *Pride and Prejudice* poster taped to her classroom wall and asked a question of the fictional Bennet sisters—Elizabeth, Jane, Mary, Catherine "Kitty," and Lydia.

"You thought dating in *your* time was tough?" she asked, eyeing each feminine face on the poster with an accusatory glare. "At least you had Darcy and Bingley taking up temporary residence in your town. And an occasional regiment of soldiers passing through to keep things interesting."

Sighing, she shut off her phone and slumped back in her chair, only to be roused by a tentative knock on her open classroom door.

"Hello?" Her friend Alexis Harper stood in the doorway, a small bouquet of wildflowers—tied with a blue bow—in her hand. Trim and blond, she wore a long ponytail with all her hair scraped away from her face. "I came to bust you out of here."

Alexis was the younger sister of Emma's best bud, Keely, who'd been successfully enticed away from Last Stand to begin a new life in Chicago with hot baseball player Nate Ramsey. Before Keely left home to enjoy life on the road with Nate, Alexis had moved from Houston to spend time with their father whose health was declining. Being a caregiver for their alcoholic dad had been more work than Alexis had suspected, making it tough to get her physical therapy practice off the ground, let alone oversee the wildflower business that she was determined to keep up in Keely's absence.

"That's the nicest thing anyone's said to me in weeks," Emma exclaimed, rising and hurrying over to hug her friend. "I was just bemoaning my fate here since it seems like everyone in town has somewhere else to be this weekend."

"Not me. I'm ready to start happy hour now if you are. It's been one of those weeks that didn't kill me, so I pray to God it made me stronger." Alexis thrust the small bundle of primroses, daisies, and Texas mountain laurel toward her. "I brought these for you now that things are starting to bloom around the house."

"They're beautiful. Thank you." Leaning over the bouquet to inhale the sweet fragrance she noticed the stems wore little caps of water to keep them from drying out. "And I'm sorry you had a rough week."

She fingered the bell-shaped mountain laurel flowers, remembering the last time anyone brought her a floral offering. It had been her homecoming corsage from Wes Ramsey, senior year. A memory that brought with it a pang since she'd been thinking of him more than usual lately now that Keely was all but engaged to Wes's older brother. But Emma had made a New Year's resolution that comparing other dating prospects with Wes Ramsey was beyond foolish. Surely, she had romanticized their old relationship because he'd been her first love. They'd been drawn to each other because they were both driven and focused on their goals with a determination that set them apart from other kids their age. But things had faltered when those goals had been so different—him chasing his baseball dream and her going to college so she could secure a job in the town she loved. But there were other men out there, and she needed to get serious about looking at them.

Sure, he was an elite athlete with an invitation to attend a major league spring training camp two weeks from now. But she'd never been a superficial woman. She'd admired his work ethic, and his innate compassion. Also, his kisses made her forget her own name. But the time had come for her to move past the fanciful wishes of her younger years, and start the search for a mate who wanted the same kind of future she did. Marriage. Family. A life in Last Stand.

"I'm sure things will get easier." Alexis wandered around the classroom, her gaze roaming from the poster of the Lady of Shalott to the heroine of *The Crucible* and, of course, the Bennet sisters. "I'm a little over my head taking care of the wildflowers. I would have never guessed there were so many farm chores this time of year. I feel like all I've been doing this week is planting and pruning." She ran a finger over the worn spines of volumes on a low bookcase. "So what do you think about happy hour?"

"I'm in." Emma dug her leather handbag out of her battered desk drawer and then locked it up again. "You can help me figure out my new dating strategy."

"Really?" Alexis looked intrigued, turning toward her with comically wide eyes. She waggled her eyebrows. "Sounds juicy. I need a distraction that doesn't involve potting trays or seeds."

"Unfortunately, my dilemma is the opposite of juicy." She grabbed her sweater off the back of her chair. "I've been staring at the same romantic candidates on my matchmaking apps for months, and I've decided to forge ahead and speed date my way through all of them to see what happens."

"Nothing like jumping in with both feet." Alexis tossed her head and laughed, ponytail swinging. "Hold that thought. This is a discussion that calls for tequila."

They drove separately to the Last Stand Saloon, a town institution and the actual spot where the settlers had made their last stand in the Texas War for Independence. Locals took pride in the place and their history, one of many reasons Emma had fallen in love with this Hill Country town when she and her vagabond mom had first settled here. The original saloon was still standing, along with bullet holes from shots fired during the battle.

For Emma, the town had lived up to its name since she'd told her roaming mother she wasn't moving again once they arrived—making a sort of last stand with her mother. To her credit, Adeline Bradford Garcia had managed to sit still long enough for Emma to finish high school, but the minute she'd headed to the University of Texas to begin her teaching degree, Adeline returned to her nomad ways.

Sliding into a booth in the back, Emma set her flowers on the table and took the seat across from Alexis. The place was already busy, the Friday happy hour starting early. While the jukebox blared an old George Jones tune, Emma waved at a few people she knew, not surprised to see a table full of the elementary school teachers toasting the start of their weekend.

"So what gives?" Alexis demanded, peeling off her sweater-coat to reveal a long-sleeved pink tee with the Windy Meadows Wildflowers logo. "Why the sudden rush to date your way through town?"

A waitress stopped by to take their drink order, interrupting Emma's answer. Afterward, she took right up where they'd left off.

"For one thing, I don't believe in wasting time," Emma said carefully, having discarded the deeper, sentimental reason as too morose. The truth was she felt lonely. And that Wes Ramsey would be leaving Last Stand for the start of baseball season soon, ending any chance meetings with him for another eight long months. It bugged her how much she still looked forward to seeing him, a sure sign she'd given him too much of her mental real estate. "I've never dated just for fun, and I'm not interested in casual hookups. I really want to stay in Last Stand, and I don't want to drive two hours to try out long-distance dates. I figured I might as well dig in and get to know potential like-minded men before I commit to another year of teaching in the fall."

"Emma, don't take this the wrong way." Alexis stabbed an emphatic finger onto the table. "But do not breathe a single word of that speech to any guy you go out with."

The server returned and set the drinks on the table along with salsa and tortilla chips, cocktail napkins and cardboard drink coasters from Outlaw Tequila, a local business. Emma lifted her longneck and clanked it against Alexis's cactus-shaped margarita glass.

"Cheers to friends who don't let friends scare away potential dates." Sipping the pilsner, Emma tried not to be discouraged. "I'll be more charming and less terrifying once I commit to the plan."

Her phone chimed with a notification on her dating app that her first prospect was suggesting an outing tomorrow night—drinks and dancing at Hickory Hall. Emma took a deep breath and sent him a thumbs-up before she lost her nerve.

"You know you shouldn't go out with men who don't inspire you in the first place?" Alexis advised, plucking a chip from the basket while the jukebox shuffled to a newer country tune with more guitar than fiddle. "You make dating sound as appealing as visiting the dentist."

Alexis smiled and waved at someone else in the bar while Emma answered her.

"Isn't it? At least, that's been my experience so far—" her experience with Wes not withstanding "—but I'm still hoping someone will surprise me." Her most recent phone call from her mom had underscored how dire her dating prospects seemed, since Adeline had suggested Emma visit Beverly Hills if she "still found herself sitting alone every Friday night with only ice cream for company."

Emma had not dignified that with a response, but the bleak description had been spot-on.

"Why are you hoping to be surprised?" The male voice

from just over Emma's shoulder was one she recognized all too well.

Wes Ramsey.

The familiar rush of awareness from seeing him made her skin heat. Had she conjured him out of her longing thoughts? He stood at the end of her bench seat, all six foot two of him with the strong shoulders of a power hitter. In faded jeans and worn boots, a blue flannel buttoned over a white T-shirt, he was dressed the same as the ranchers and locals that populated Last Stand Saloon. But his dark hair, green eyes, and chiseled jaw were so familiar to her. She'd kissed that mouth more times than she could count and still not often enough to satisfy her.

"Do you mind if we join you for a couple of minutes?" the guy behind Wes asked, making her aware Wes wasn't alone. His friend dropped into the bench seat beside Alexis. "The place is packed."

Ty Lambert had been a fixture on the Houston Stars roster for the last few years, even though he'd been hurt in a motorcycle accident last season. Emma had seen Ty a few times at the baseball camp Wes's brother, Nate, started last summer while recovering from an injury. Ty had volunteered too, bringing star power to the camp and ensuring the venture was a huge success. Emma had heard Ty was sweet on Alexis, making extra trips to Last Stand even after the baseball camp ended, but Emma hadn't seen the two of them together until now.

Alexis gave a flirty laugh, her eyes lighting up at the sight of him. "As long as the next round is on you." She scooted deeper into the bench seat to make room for him. His deeply bronzed skin made his pale, blue-green eyes stand out all the more. His dark hair fell across one eye, the ink of a few tattoos visible above the collar of a gray button-down he wore with his jeans. To Emma, Alexis said, "You've met Ty Lambert before haven't you?"

Emma offered her hand across the table, trying to focus on Ty and not the rush of awareness that came as Wes took a seat beside her. "Emma Garcia. I saw you at the Stars camp a few times this summer."

"Nice to meet you. I knew you looked familiar," Ty said before the server returned to take their drink order.

Wes and Ty ordered beers and Alexis asked for a second margarita, but Emma declined. She couldn't afford to dull her wits with Wes next to her. They'd crossed paths a handful of times during the off-season, but hadn't spoken beyond pleasantries. And they certainly hadn't been in such close proximity since their breakup the summer after freshman year of college.

A break taken for sensible reasons since Emma guessed that Wes would get drafted before he finished his four-year degree. She'd recognized it wouldn't be fair to tie him down when he was launching a career that would have him traveling all over the country, being pursued by rabid fangirls. They'd pretended the split had been amicable, but there'd been plenty of heartache beneath the surface on her side. Wes told her he understood, and sharpened his focus on baseball. Emma had sobbed her eyes out and bitterly regretted her inability to live in the moment.

"Emma, we'll give you space as soon as a spot opens up at the bar," Ty assured her as their server left the table. "Alexis won't thank me for cutting in on her friend time."

"You're fine," Emma insisted, forcing herself to relax back against the seat cushion. "We're just celebrating the start of the weekend. And, for me, two whole days' respite from writing up learning outcomes and justifying teaching objectives."

She loved teaching and working with her students, but the emphasis on testing in the school system frustrated her to no end.

"You're a teacher?" Ty asked at the same time laughter erupted at a table nearby.

"Ninth-grade English," she said, before steering talk away from her work. "Which isn't nearly as interesting as what you do. I'm sure you're looking forward to training camp."

Ty shrugged as he cut eyes toward Alexis. "Actually, I'll miss hanging out in Last Stand when I leave for Palm Beach."

Ty's Houston-based team trained in Florida while all the Ramsey men would attend spring training in Arizona. Cal and Nate in Mesa, and Wes in Scottsdale. *The Defender*, the local newspaper, had spelled that out in their sports section last week, along with updates on the local bull riders.

The server returned with their drinks, and Emma noticed

Ty used the interruption to speak privately with Alexis.

Wes turned toward Emma and lowered his voice. "Ty might be indifferent, but I'm definitely ready to go to camp."

She couldn't help the stab of disappointment that he was eager to leave town even though she'd always known a spot on a major league roster was his goal.

"You've worked hard for this chance, Wes." She fidgeted with the bow tied around the bouquet that Alexis had given her—a bouquet she'd brought into the bar to flaunt and maybe boost her friend's flower business. She wanted to be better about supporting local entrepreneurs. "Congratulations on getting the invitation."

"Thanks. But it's not going to be easy getting on the roster. Their second baseman has two Gold Gloves." He took a drink of his beer before eyeing the label from a local brewery.

"According to your dad, they could put you in left field." Emma glanced toward Alexis to check in with her friend, but Ty had her smiling. There was definitely a spark between them.

"Why am I not surprised you've heard my father's views about my potential position?" Wes asked dryly.

Clint Ramsey had a long, storied career as a major league pitcher and had passed his baseball skills to all three of his sons. But Cal, Nate, and Wes also dealt with their dad's criticisms. Their mom had given Clint his walking papers long ago, and the Hall of Famer now lived in a mansion across town with a superficial gold digger who'd once told Emma that she should have really set her sights on someone with a more *established* baseball career than Wes. As if the goal was the income and not the man.

But Wes had borne far worse growing up in the Ramsey household, between the constant pressure to improve his game and the need to win his father's approval that always remained just out of reach. Sometimes she'd wondered if Wes pursued his dream for himself or because it seemed to be expected, but if she'd learned one thing about him while they were dating, it's that he wouldn't put the dream aside for anything. So, regretfully, she'd stepped away on her own terms before that drive of his ripped him out of her arms for good.

"He was holding court during the tree trimming at the Corbyn family's mansion before Christmas," Emma recalled before she took another sip of the pilsner. "But it wasn't just to talk about you. He was giving everyone updates on Nate and Cal, too."

Wes's jaw flexed and she guessed that his tense relationship with his father hadn't eased over the years.

"On to more interesting subjects," Wes spoke more loudly when Ty and Alexis went quiet on the other side of the table, including them in the conversation even though his green eyes remained on Emma. "I heard you say you hoped someone would surprise you when we first got here." A teasing note entered his voice. "What was that all about?"

Alexis leaned closer, her pendant of a silver rose banging the table as she grinned. "This is a good story. Emma, you should run the plan by the guys and get their take on it."

"It's not really a story I planned to share." She glared at Alexis meaningfully while Wes swiveled in his seat to face Emma more.

"Now I'm intrigued," he said, drumming his fingers against the tabletop. The wood vibrated under her elbows. "What are you up to?"

Alexis dipped a chip in salsa, adding, "It's not like your scheme will remain a secret if you opt to move forward with it."

Sighing, Emma couldn't deny her friend had a point. News traveled fast in a small town.

"Fine." She sipped her beer and reminded herself she had no reason to be embarrassed even though Wes probably had women throwing themselves at him daily while she struggled to meet anyone. "I'm thinking about speed dating my way through the only prospects that show up on my dating app to get an idea of whether or not I can afford to spend another year in Last Stand."

Ty's eyebrows shot up. Wes frowned.

"Let me get this straight." Narrowing his gaze, Wes spoke coolly. "You'd actually consider leaving Last Stand if there are no good romantic candidates?"

She nodded.

Ty slapped the table with his palm and said, "Brilliant. Emma, I think you're on to something. Why stay in a geographic area with no prospects? If you were a wild animal, you'd move to a new hunting ground. This is no different."

Wes shook his head, a lock of dark hair spilling onto his

forehead. "It's very different since Emma is a woman and not a wolf. She can't change her whole life just because the dating pool isn't up to her standards."

She bristled at his words. Or maybe it was how he said them. As if she was being overly picky.

"It's not really that," she clarified. "I just don't want to waste time dating someone who doesn't want the same things as me. And I'm not interested in a long-distance relationship. So I figured I'd better get to work and see if there's anyone out there in Last Stand for me."

"And if not?" Wes's jaw flexed, the dark shadow of stubble shifting with the movement. "You'd honestly move away just to find better dates?"

He made it sound frivolous.

Self-indulgent.

So of course she committed to the plan all the more. "Absolutely."

They stared at one another under the yellow glow from an overhead pendant. Ty reaffirmed that he thought it was a good idea. Wes didn't speak. So when the tune on the jukebox changed to something slow, Ty slid out of the booth and beckoned to Alexis.

"Come on, Alexis. Let me show you my dance moves." Ty drew her toward the planked dance floor, weaving through patrons that crowded the area behind the bar.

Once they were gone, Wes scowled at Emma while he finished his beer in silence.

Twitchy and anxious at being alone with him, Emma

pulled her flowers to her nose to inhale the fragrance, taking comfort from them since one Harper sister had planted them and the other one had picked them for Emma. With the aromatherapy soothing her nerves, she decided to say what was on her mind since she most likely wouldn't be seeing Wes again before he left town.

And if she decided to leave Last Stand for greener dating pastures, she'd move in the summer before he finished the baseball season. The thought of never seeing him again unsettled her, even though they'd split long ago.

"So I take it you think it's a bad idea?" She tried to keep her voice light since it was just idle conversation. She made her own decisions.

"I didn't say that," he replied slowly, withdrawing his wallet and tucking a few bills under his empty beer bottle. "I just find it ironic that you wouldn't consider leaving Last Stand while we were together, and I was entering the draft. But now you're ready to pack your bags for the sake of a date. Guess it shows where I ranked."

Rising to his feet, Wes wished her a good night while she tried to process what he'd just said. By the time she did, he was walking his very fine self right out the door.

Indignation had her out of the booth, her purse and flowers in hand. She'd never been the kind of woman to chase a man, but if Wes thought he could make a pronouncement like that and then walk away from her, he didn't know her at all.

Chapter Two

WALKING DOWN MAIN Street toward his pickup, Wes Ramsey tried to clear his head by dragging in deep breaths of the cool night air. He had less than two weeks left in Last Stand before he launched the next phase of his baseball career and he couldn't afford to get distracted by Emma Garcia, no matter how smoking hot she looked tonight. Or how much he hated the idea of her dating her way through Last Stand. She'd already made it clear to him that his lifestyle didn't match with hers. Lesson learned the hard way. So now, he needed to focus on his job. He'd worked tirelessly to get onto a major league roster, devoting himself to the cause from the time he was old enough to remember wanting anything. The need to claim his spot had been bred into him.

His father had been a pitching coach after he'd retired as a player, unable to tear himself away from the sport. But after Clint Ramsey sat on the sidelines during Wes's first T-ball game and had—according to one of the many interviews Clint had given on the subject—"seen the quality of his youngest son's swing," he'd given up his job to devote himself to coaching his own sons. Wes's older brothers claimed they recalled a few years of normalcy before that day. Their childhoods had involved a tree house. Some farm chores. Life outside baseball. But Wes couldn't remember a time without daily skills drills.

He'd sacrificed everything for his dad and the family dream. Including the sexy redhead he'd walked away from inside Last Stand Saloon.

Reaching his truck, a stripped-down beater that he refused to trade in until he shook off the dust of the minor leagues for good, Wes was unlocking the driver's side door when the rapid tattoo of boots on tarmac made him look up.

Emma charged toward him, a short, peacock-blue sweater draped over her shoulders, while dark leggings showed off her memorable legs. Her auburn hair had grown longer in the last year, from the razor-sharp cut that ended at her chin, to curls that now rested on her shoulders. A rhinestone comb glinted under a streetlight, and for some reason seeing the old-fashioned piece of jewelry reminded him of how she'd identified her style for him once. Flea-market glamour, she'd called it. The memory almost made him smile even though Emma looked like she was gunning for bear, her lightly glossed lips puckered into a frown.

"Miss me already?" he asked, pocketing his keys as she crossed the courthouse parking lot.

When the bar filled up, the courthouse made an easy overflow lot one block over. He'd already spotted Emma's car there too. Like him, she'd kept the same vehicle forever. Beneath her quirky fashion style, she was a practical woman.

Or so he'd thought until she'd unveiled her dating scheme. The idea of her checking off the town's bachelors like a game show contestant rankled.

"I wouldn't call it 'missing you' when you dropped a gauntlet then disappeared before I had the chance to respond." She juggled her purse and her flowers into one hand as she stopped beside his front tire.

They were alone in this part of the parking lot, the downtown quiet at this time of night except for a handful of people outside the bar.

"A gauntlet?" He scrubbed a hand over his unshaven jaw and wondered how she still got under his skin with her English-teacher-speak and her flea-market rhinestones. "I'm pretty sure I didn't drop any such thing, Emma. Just making an observation."

"A very incorrect one," she insisted, wrapping her bright sweater tighter around herself. "I never said I wouldn't leave Last Stand when you were entering the draft."

She tilted her chin at him, her heart-shaped face so damned familiar even after all this time. He remembered kissing the freckles across her nose. Tucking that brilliant auburn hair behind her ear. Cataloging the things that made a dimple appear in her left cheek. A polite smile wasn't enough for it to show up. But laughter or a real, from-the-gut grin carved the small divot there.

"The whole reason we split was so you wouldn't have to leave Last Stand," he reminded her, the words deliberately mild even though her abrupt defection during a time of huge change in his life had thrown him for a loop.

She shook her head, the cinnamon-colored curls dancing. "How can you say that? I set you free so you could pursue your lifelong dream without feeling tied down."

The sincerity in her voice suggested she really believed what she said. He wondered how they could have come away with such different views of what went down that day.

"I never asked to be set free though, did I?" He leaned a shoulder against his truck door, giving in to the desire to stare at her while blocking out the rest of the world behind them. "You bailed before we had a chance to talk about the future."

She shuffled from foot to foot, biting her lip before she looked down. Because she was unsure of herself? Or to keep from saying something that was on her mind?

He waited, trying not to remember the days where he would have answered her unease by reeling her closer and kissing her until she relaxed against him. Raised by an impulsive and irresponsible single mother, Emma had been the grown-up in her household even when she was in high school, and he knew a lot of pressure had come with that. He'd gravitated toward her because he'd recognized someone else who hadn't had a childhood. Someone carrying a heavier than normal burden for a high schooler.

"I never said I wouldn't leave Last Stand," she said finally, picking her head up to meet his gaze. "I just didn't want to be an anchor for you when you needed to direct your energy toward your dream."

A flicker of surprise went through him. He hadn't remembered it that way at all.

"At the time, maybe I was too shell-shocked to hear what you were saying," he acknowledged, certain he hadn't been at his best once he'd understood she was trying to tell him it was over. He'd returned to Last Stand that summer full of plans for how they could make their relationship work while he was in the minors, but that discussion had never happened once Emma launched into her explanation for why they shouldn't keep seeing each other.

"You had a lot on your mind." Her blue eyes roamed over him. "People who write off professional sports as 'just a game' have no idea how much preparation is involved to get there."

The understanding—in both her words and her expression—reminded him of another thing he'd loved about her. But she'd thrown his love away while assuming she knew best. He locked down the what-ifs and might-have-beens since they didn't matter right now. He needed to leave well enough alone now that the stakes had never been higher for his career.

"Not to mention how many people put in the preparation and never make it." He'd known plenty of guys who'd fallen away from the sport they loved because they couldn't make ends meet on the small income paid to minor leaguers, or couldn't ask their loved ones to make the sacrifices of time spent apart while the players were on the road.

"That won't happen to you." The certainty in her words,

her belief in him, meant more to him than it probably should. "Your brothers have always said you were the one destined to have the biggest career of all of them, and they're already playing at that level."

"We'll see." He should be thrilled about the upcoming opportunity. His teammates in the minors had all been happy for him. But even now, the pressure was too great to stop and enjoy any sense of achievement. "In the meantime, I have no business weighing in on your dating life, even if I happen to think it's a bad idea."

With her wry laugh, her breath huffed in a white cloud in the cold air. "You have no business telling me, but you'll tell me anyway?"

He shrugged. Words had never been his strong suit. "I guess you should consider the source, is all. I'm hardly an expert on dating, but why use an app when you're only looking at the guys in town? You already know them all. Either you like someone, or you don't."

"Just because Mike Daughtry use to pull my hair when he was in the third grade doesn't mean I know him that well. People change." She shivered and hugged herself tighter. "I know I have."

Daughtry? His stomach dropped at the thought. The guy wasn't even close to good enough for her.

"You're cold," he observed, regretting that they were having this conversation in a parking lot, especially as an older couple waved to them before getting into their sedan in the next row. "Do you want to talk in the truck? I can turn the heat on."

He needed more time to convince her this scheme of hers was unwise. Or to at least steer her away from the worst of her potential dates.

Appearing to consider the offer, Emma eyed the red Ford. He wondered if she was remembering kisses they'd shared on that bench seat. He sure as hell was.

"That's okay. I shouldn't keep you." She backed up a step, the pink in her cheeks deepening. "And I shouldn't bail on Alexis without saying good night."

He wanted to argue the point, but what right did he have to offer opinions on her life now? With more than a little regret, he nodded.

"All right. But I hope you'll remember how much you've always loved living in Last Stand. I think you'd be sorry to leave." He didn't like the thought of her not being here. They might not have spoken much in the last few years, but he remembered all the efforts she'd made to convince her mom to stay for her senior year when Adeline had wanted to pull up stakes.

Emma had told him that it felt like home. At the time, he'd imagined a future with her in it. He'd envisioned her on the road with him, but returning in the off-season to a place they both loved no matter how far away their future carried them.

"I'm sure I would be," she admitted, a sad smile curving her lips, but then it faded, replaced by a determined gleam in her eyes. "But I won't put off my future indefinitely."

He ground his teeth together, but still failed to restrain a final word of warning.

"Just do me a favor and scratch Mike Daughtry off your list." The idea of her sharing appetizers and making small talk with a mealy-mouthed guy like that was too much for his peace of mind. "He's not worthy of you."

The smile she gave him was the first genuine one he'd seen from her all night. The dimple flashed, and he wanted to track the small indent with his finger before it faded.

"Thanks for the tip, Wes." She backed up another step. "And good luck in Arizona if I don't see you again."

She was already hurrying back toward the bar when it occurred to him she hadn't agreed to stay away from the guy. Disgruntled and out of sorts, he told himself it didn't matter.

He'd done his civic duty where Emma Garcia was concerned. For now, that had to be enough.

IT'S NOT LIKE Emma had *planned* to ignore Wes's warning, she thought to herself with a hint of guilt the next night as she sat across from local CPA Mike Daughtry at a corner table in the back of Hickory Hall.

The local dance hall was crowded for a live show from a popular country band, a few windows opened on the sides of the building letting the cool night air inside along with the scent of pine trees and damp earth from the creek nearby. She'd driven separately for her first date with Mike, something she'd already been in the process of arranging before Wes had tried to steer her away from him. Now, she sipped her beer slowly, enjoying the music even though the venue made it difficult to get to know her date better.

Not that it discouraged Mike from talking loudly while the band played, speaking animatedly about his online accounting business that brought him more work than his local clients. She felt her eyes glaze over just a little at his detailed discussion, but she knew she could get equally wrapped up when she spoke about the Brontës' novels, so she could hardly fault him for being passionate about his job. He looked around the dance hall often, and she wondered if he was expecting to see someone elsc here or if he was just a distracted speaker.

Mind wandering as he spoke, Emma tapped her foot to the two-step song while she took her date's measure. He'd graduated from Creekbend High two years before her, so she hadn't known him well, but she had a few memories of him. The hair-pulling had been in grade school, so she'd been honest when she told Wes that she didn't hold that against him. She'd seen Mike run track once and recalled that he had a few girlfriends. She had the impression he'd been well liked, even if he'd seemed a little full of himself. Tonight, he wore jeans and boots with a dark red dress shirt. His light brown hair was cut well, and he was good-looking enough. There wasn't anything objectionable about him that she could see—despite Wes's warning. Yet that didn't stop her from finding Mike wanting when she compared him to Wes.

Which wasn't fair. Not to herself, and definitely not to her date. But seeing Wes last night had stirred up old feelings, making it next to impossible to enjoy what should have been an entertaining evening.

Even though Mike seemed ready to talk his way through the band's next number, too.

Waiting for him to take a breath, she spoke quickly when he finally paused.

"So you plan to stay in Last Stand long term?" she asked, mentally clicking through the list of questions she'd come up with to help her learn more about her dates. "It sounds as if you're doing well here."

"Well? Yes, I'd say so." With a smile bordering on smugness, he lifted his beer as if toasting himself, then took a drink. "For that matter, my business is expanding so fast that I could work from anywhere in the world." He leaned over the table, crowding her. "Is there any place in particular you'd want to see?"

Leaning back in her seat, she managed to reclaim some personal space and told herself that plenty of people took pride in their work accomplishments. That wasn't necessarily a bad thing. Although she could do without him trying to speed his way toward physical closeness.

"I traveled a lot before I moved here." She'd been in every state before she was ten. "I'm still enjoying the chance to stay in one place."

It was the first time he'd asked her anything about herself.

"You were a kid then," he scoffed with a dismissive air, glancing around the dance hall for the umpteenth time. "That's hardly traveling when you weren't at the helm, making your own choices."

She had a reply on the tip of her tongue, but he spoke on top of her.

"You need to see the world, Emma. You need to live a little." He returned his gaze to her again, pointing his beer bottle at her for emphasis.

She bit her tongue against a rude retort, realizing that she couldn't talk herself into liking the man across from her. She refused to waste an evening with someone who barely gave her room to speak, and then didn't care about her opinions even when she finally got a chance to voice them.

"I think I'm a better judge of what I need," she said tightly, wondering how fast she could finish her beer so she could excuse herself.

Her date sucked in a breath as if to unleash another three-song diatribe when a shadow fell over her beer.

"Would you care to dance?" a familiar masculine voice asked from over her shoulder.

Her breath caught.

She glanced up into Wes Ramsey's green eyes for the second time in as many days.

And even though Wes's expression was deeply scowling, she was grateful to see him. Because why should she continue to make polite conversation with the man sharing her table when he couldn't be bothered to extend her common courtesy?

"I'd like that," she told Wes, already tucking the thin strap of her cross-body handbag over her shoulder. Then, turning back to Mike, she smiled sweetly. "I'm going to go live a little. Thank you for the advice."

She might have taken more satisfaction from her exit if Mike hadn't already been gathering up his keys and wallet. He gave her a nod before he walked away.

A nod.

Sighing over her own folly at trying to see something redeeming in Mike that wasn't there, she took Wes's hand as she stood.

"You tried to warn me," she admitted, feeling a hum of awareness all through her as Wes folded her fingers in his palm. "I might have listened too, if I hadn't already agreed to meet him here tonight."

"You didn't notice him keeping one eye on the door to make sure his girlfriend didn't show up?" Wes asked before he tugged her through the crowd toward the dance floor.

Stunned, Emma hastened her step to keep up with him. "He has a *girlfriend*?"

Reaching the patch of planked floor used for dancing, Wes waited for a break in the two-stepping couples before he pulled her into his arms. The feel of Wes's hand on the back of her shoulder soothed the rankled feeling inside her as they fell into the steps, moving counterclockwise around the floor.

"Maybe not, but since that's been his M.O. forever, it's a reasonable assumption," Wes muttered darkly. "It's a small town, Emma. I'm surprised you hadn't heard."

Mike's request that they take the back table made perfect sense now. As did his need to keep glancing around the room.

"I guess I haven't been tuned in to the right gossip." She wasn't that upset about the dating mishap, however, considering her left arm rested lightly along Wes's right, her fingers on his shoulder. "Are you here with friends?"

"Cal and I came to have a drink and listen to the band while we sort through what to do about the farm." A line of worry deepened between his brows as he spoke about Rough Hollow Farm and Orchards, a business run by their grandfather, Everett Ramsey. "Granddad's not getting any younger, and we've got to figure out if we're going to sell the place or hire someone to take over on a larger scale."

"I have such good memories of the farmhouse." Wes's mother, Hailey Decker, still lived in the home where she'd raised her sons, next door to her former father-in-law, Everett. Wes had divided his time between his father's new mansion on one side of town and his mom's place, but both she and Wes had liked the farmhouse more. Plus, his mother was an easygoing, warmhearted woman who always made Emma feel welcome. "I can't imagine having Rough Hollow run by anyone but a Ramsey."

The line between Wes's brows deepened. But before he could reply, it occurred to her she might be keeping him from his brother.

"Is Cal waiting for you?" She missed a step of the dance

and had to shuffle to catch up. "I don't want to interrupt your time together."

"No." Wes's expression eased. "He got a text from his fiancée, Josie, and took off right before I saw you with Mike."

She relaxed a fraction, glad she wasn't keeping him from his family. Because selfishly, it felt good to be in Wes's arms tonight, even if dancing was as far as things could go between them.

She knew better than to get her hopes up where this professional wanderer was concerned. He was leaving Last Stand in less than two weeks.

"Well thanks for coming over to my table." She owed him that much. "I was just realizing that I needed to bail on him when you arrived."

The song ended and they clapped along with the rest of the crowd, on and off the dance floor.

"Good for you." He steered her away from the dance floor over toward the pool tables as the next song began. "But there's no need to end your evening prematurely since I'm free, too. Want to take a walk by the water?" He nodded toward the side door that led out to the parking area and the woods and creek beyond. "I have a coat in my truck if you need one."

She debated the wisdom of spending more time with a man who still affected her the way Wes did. Then again, hadn't she just decided she knew better than to get her hopes up where he was concerned?

The feel of his hands still warmed her skin everywhere he'd touched her during their dance. So, whether it was wise or not, she found herself nodding, unwilling to walk away from him just yet.

"Let's go." Heart beating faster, she followed him out of the dance hall and into a chilly Texas night full of possibility.

Chapter Three

NORMALLY, WES THOUGHT things through before he made decisions. He listed pros and cons. He slept on a choice to see how he felt about it in the morning.

But all that careful decision-making had gone out the window as soon as he'd spied Emma sitting across from the local two-timer. He'd charged toward her without a plan, without a care for how it looked to interrupt her date. He'd simply known he wanted her away from Daughtry as fast as possible. He wondered if he would have been as quick to interrupt her evening if she'd been with anyone else. Had he reacted to seeing her with someone he didn't like? Or would seeing her with anyone get under his skin?

They'd broken up so long ago that he didn't want to think the latter. But then again, he'd never been tested before when it came to this woman. Any time he'd seen Emma around town in the off-season, she'd been alone or with girlfriends.

Now, after retrieving his jacket for her from his truck, Wes slid the flannel-lined, oilskin coat around her shoulders to keep her warm for their walk. She'd dressed in jeans and some kind of flowery tunic for the night, but at least the black combat boots—a funky choice with the feminine top—were good for walking by the creek's edge.

"Here you go." He wanted to smooth the collar flat around her neck, but since that was only a bid to touch her, he forced his hands into his pockets. The fabric of his coat reached almost to her knees, but she drew the sides together and tucked it around her. He couldn't help the fierce sense of satisfaction that came from one small act of caring for her.

"This is perfect. Thank you." She followed him out the back of the parking lot toward the long slope that led down to Hickory Creek.

The path through the trees was dark as they walked farther from the white lights around Hickory Hall, so Wes took his time leading the way, reaching back now and again to give Emma a hand over rocky spots. When the sound of the rushing water grew louder than the music filtering out the open windows of the dance hall, he led Emma along the path near the water. Sometimes other people found their way down here at night, but perhaps because of the cool weather, Wes and Emma were alone in the moonlight under a clear sky.

He glanced over at her face that looked even paler in the dim moon glow. She peered up through the dark branches of a leafless tree, the long column of her neck exposed above the collar of the jacket. Being alone with her again after all this time was messing with his head, reminding him of how much they'd been to one another once. Or maybe it was hearing her explanation of her motive for breaking things off with him when they'd spoken last night. His whole perception of their split had changed since they'd talked. He'd thought she'd ended things because of her desire to stay in Last Stand when she knew he could be on the road for years to come.

But according to her, she hadn't wanted him to feel tied down. All of which had churned around his brain last night, leading him to the talk he wished to have with her now.

"I hope tonight's fiasco makes you reevaluate your dating strategy." He came straight to the point as they wove around a stump where a tree had fallen across the creek.

"Not at all," she shot back quickly as she stepped over a tree root. "My whole intention is to check out people I'm supposed to be compatible with in the area. My strategy is working if I'm already crossing someone off the list."

Frustrated, he ground his teeth at the thought of her out every weekend to interrogate a new guy. "Doesn't that seem a little bloodless?"

They were almost to the end of the good path. Ahead of them, a more densely wooded area loomed up a short incline.

She laughed dryly, running her fingers through her hair in a way that drew his eye. "Possibly. But I'm not patient enough to sit around waiting for life to happen to me. I won't spend another year teaching in Last Stand if there's no hope of a future and family for me here." She slowed her step as they came to the end of the moonlit section of the trail. "Tonight wasn't fun, but it helped me make progress."

Wes stopped, reaching for her elbow to draw her attention to him. To what he wanted to say.

"I have a better proposition for you." He looked into her blue eyes.

The fog of their mingled breaths drifted between them.

Her eyebrow arched as she met his gaze. "I'm listening."

He decided to appeal to her relentlessly practical nature. "Add my name to your list."

For a moment, there was no sound except for the gurgle of the creek and a call of a night bird.

Emma frowned. "Excuse me?"

His gaze moved to her lips. The urge to kiss away her puzzled expression was undeniable.

"Give me a spot on the dating roster," he clarified, a list of reasons at the ready if he needed to defend the request. "I can't be any worse than Daughtry, and he got a try-out."

"You can't be serious," she told him flatly, already shaking her head. Her curls grazed the shoulders of his jacket, sweeping back and forth with the motion. "You leave in less than two weeks."

He'd never been good at backing down when challenged, so her words only fueled his certainty.

"On the contrary, I'm very serious. And you gave Daughtry his walking papers after one beer, so two weeks should be plenty of time for you to get to know me."

"I already know you." She folded her arms, the extra bulk of his coat shifting around her smaller frame.

"You told me last night that people change. That *you've*

changed." He hadn't forgotten her words when she'd tried to justify why she felt comfortable reconnecting with people she'd known in her youth. "So maybe we don't know each other as well as you think."

Her blue eyes were gray in the moonlight as they widened in surprise. "We dated for two and a half years."

"In high school and college." He'd had a lot on his plate then to ensure the jump to university with a strong baseball program. "We were only half-formed into the adults we would become."

She fidgeted with the tab on the front of his coat, tipping it back and forth while she seemed to consider this. The white haze of her breath clung to her in a ghostly outline. "Why would you want to revisit a past that already ended painfully for us?"

It was the first indication that the split had hurt her, too. For years afterward, he'd thought she only wanted to protect herself by breaking things off when he entered the draft. He hadn't known it had cost her, too.

Unable to stop himself, he reached for her, resting his hands on her shoulders.

"Because hearing about your plan to date your way through town felt wrong to me," he told her honestly, skimming his palms down her forearms. "And I don't ignore my instincts."

He might be a practical and driven man. But that didn't mean he dismissed his hunches when he had a strong feeling about something. And every impulse he possessed urged him to spend more time with Emma Garcia.

"But my whole point in the dating scheme is to find someone I have chemistry with—"

"That's definitely not a problem," he reminded her, taking her hands in his, all too prepared to remind her of the sparks they generated just by breathing the same air.

"*And*," she continued as if he hadn't interrupted, "someone who is local. I already know you're leaving, so you don't fit the bill."

She didn't withdraw her fingers from his, and it took all his willpower not to kiss her. Instead, he contented himself with spinning one of her silver rings around her finger. He needed to appeal to her brain or the rest of her wouldn't get on board.

"But you also said you'd leave Last Stand if you didn't find someone in town." He'd listened to her carefully last night and he'd formulated his pitch accordingly.

"I meant it." She tilted her chin at him, as if defying him to contradict her.

"So if *you'd* leave Last Stand, then you can't rule me out. You could come on the road with me."

This time, she did pull her hands from his. Then, she stuffed them in the pockets of the borrowed coat for good measure.

"We're getting ahead of ourselves." She shuffled from foot to foot. "Maybe we should go back."

"Sure." He turned with her to retrace their steps. As they walked, he could see the lights from the dance hall now and then through the trees. "And I agree we're getting ahead of ourselves. Why don't we just set up a date and see how it goes?"

"What if we only make it through one beer?" She gave him a sideways glance, a wicked gleam in her eyes.

"Then at least I had my shot." He held up his hands in surrender. "If I can't entertain you longer than two-timing Mike, I don't deserve your company for more than one drink."

"We're going to set local tongues wagging," she observed as she stepped around the roots of the fallen tree.

He smiled at the old-fashioned expression while he kept a hand close to her elbow in case she slipped. "I think you were bound to do that with or without my help."

"Probably." She didn't sound too concerned about it. "But will you have time to do something this week? I thought you and Cal had things to work through for the farming business before you leave."

The reminder of it made his shoulders tense. Every option they came up with got shot down by Granddad.

"I can do both. In fact, I'll need to balance the frustration of the farming worries with some kind of outlet." He couldn't afford to show up at training camp without his head in the game. One way or another, he had to hash out a plan for the family business since his father had never wanted anything to do with it.

He couldn't let his grandfather down.

Maybe some of his worry was evident in his voice, because Emma tucked her hand in the crook of his elbow as they started up the hill toward the parking lot.

"You'll figure something out," she assured him, her voice steady while the sound of steel guitars drifted on the breeze.

"I hope so." He halted his step before they could return to the activity around the dance hall.

He could hear laughter and conversation spilling out of the venue into the picnic area and parking lot beyond. Emma stopped beside him, peering up at him curiously.

"What is it?" She clearly wondered why he hadn't continued toward his truck.

"I just wanted to be sure we're in agreement. I get at least one date?" He couldn't resist the urge to swipe a copper-colored curl from her cheek.

"Yes." She nodded. "You've got your spot on the dating roster."

"Excellent." Satisfaction fired through him. His competitive nature wouldn't allow him to fail. "We just need to seal the deal."

"My word isn't good enough?"

"A kiss is customary." His gaze dipped to her beautifully shaped mouth.

Full and soft, with a pronounced cupid's bow in the upper lip.

"You're thinking of a handshake." She extended her hand toward him.

"No." He gripped some of the excess fabric of the coat and tugged her—slowly—toward him. "I'm definitely thinking of a kiss. It's all I can think about."

"The kiss only happens after the date." Her voice was breathless, her focus darting from his eyes to his mouth. "And only if it's a successful one."

"You've given this far too much thought, Emma." He wondered if she tasted the way he remembered. If she still made a tiny sigh of surrender after the first few seconds of a good kiss.

He'd loved that moment. Waited for it. Savored it.

"Good kisses are worth thinking about." She met his gaze. Held it.

And it nearly killed him to release the fabric of the coat. Admit she had a point.

"That's all I'll be thinking about then," he assured her, trying to keep the growl out of his voice and only half succeeding.

"In that case, you should set up the date soon." Her gaze lingered, and he wondered if she was mesmerized by the idea of kissing him, too.

The possibility tantalized him.

"Depend on it." He appreciated the reminder not to take this date lightly. He'd won a try-out, and he had every intention of making it count.

❧

EMMA RAN ERRANDS around town the next day with her neighbor's Siberian retriever mix, Sasha, in the back seat of her SUV. Emma frequently served as a dog-sitter for other teachers and friends when they went out of town since she liked dogs and had a fenced yard but no pets. Not committing to a dog of her own seemed like another way she'd put off her own life while waiting for the family she dreamed about.

No more delaying her happiness, damn it. Maybe getting her own dog would have been a better warm-up to a family than searching for Mr. Right on a dating app.

But for today, she'd taken Sasha on a walk around the park in downtown after grabbing coffee and a pastry—plus a homemade dog treat—at Hildie's Haus, the local diner. Then Emma had shopped for her mother's birthday present, never an easy task since Adeline always built up occasions in her mind until there was no way the reality could live up to her hopes.

Now, as she and Sasha headed back home, Emma found herself driving on the south side of town. Close to the storefront for Rough Hollow Farm and Orchards. It hadn't been a conscious decision. But the new direction hardly surprised her given how much Wes Ramsey had been in her thoughts.

Along with the kiss she hadn't indulged down by Hickory Creek last night.

Outside the SUV window, acres of farmland gave way to peach trees on a property she'd once known well. The farmhouse wasn't in view of the roadside stand. The business had been kept separate from the family's home life. But she'd spent time in these orchards with Wes when they'd dated, walking the picturesque lanes between the older, bigger trees or riding on the back of one of the four-wheelers to spend time by Hickory Creek.

When the painted sign for Rough Hollow Farm and Orchards came into view now, she hit the brakes.

"Wes wouldn't be around the farm stand now anyhow," she speculated aloud to Sasha, whose tail banged the back seat rhythmically at being included in conversation. "So it's not like I was trying to see him today. It's been years since I've been inside the place."

And she was curious about it after Wes mentioned there was a chance they would sell the business. She'd always liked his gruff grandfather, Everett Ramsey, and his mom, Hailey Decker, who ran a small beekeeping operation on the farm.

Parking the car in front of the roadside stand alongside half a dozen other vehicles, Emma got out and opened the rear door to unhook Sasha's harness. After clipping on the leash, Emma stood back so the dog could leap to the ground. Ready to explore, she locked the vehicle and headed toward the low log building with a planked porch, the double doors open wide to let in the fresh air on the mild day.

Baskets of flowers hung from wires strung across a pergola in front of the farm stand. A big barn loomed in back, with a couple of hay wagons and two tractors parked in outbuildings nearby. A red gingham tablecloth draped over a barrel showcased jars of locally bottled honey, jam and cane syrup. Bushels of turnips, radishes and beets filled a wooden display shelf, with chalkboards labeling the varieties.

A young couple emerged through the open doors, carrying a bundle of spinach and a few bunches of parsley. Emma strode closer to the building for a better look at the homemade offerings when she heard a raised voice from within.

"Confound it, I'm old but I'm not an invalid," a scratchy male voice accused, the sentiment punctuated by the stamp of something. A foot? Or a fist on a table, maybe? "I can make my own way outside, for pity's sake."

The last part was spoken more quietly, the muttered grumble mingling with the electronic chime of a cash register, and the low conversation of other patrons drifting through the open doors.

Emma encouraged Sasha nearer to her to keep the dog well clear of the entrance as a shuffling sound grew louder. A moment later, a walker rolled out onto the planked porch, followed by a scowling older gentleman dressed in work pants and a pinstriped button-down shirt left open at the neck. His thin white hair blew upright in the breeze as he rolled over to a wooden Adirondack chair full of cushions on the far side of the porch.

For a moment, Emma hadn't identified the old man since he was much thinner than she remembered. But as recognition kicked in, so did a sense of foreboding.

"Mr. Ramsey?" She moved closer to Wes's grandfather before he answered, thinking the Adirondack chair looked precariously low for someone moving so stiffly. Keeping Sasha on her left, she extended her right hand toward Everett

Ramsey, ready to steady him if he faltered. "Emma Garcia," she reminded him when his sharp gaze landed on her, looking a bit blank. "Nice to see you again."

The man nodded slowly. "So it is. Good to see you, too." He let go of his walker and took the arm she offered. "And you're just in time to save an old man from losing face. It's one thing to take help from a pretty girl. Another thing entirely to let my own grandsons hover about me like I've already got a foot in the grave."

Grandsons?

Her gaze darted toward the open doors of the farm stand, but only for a split second, since she had no intention of letting Mr. Ramsey fall on her watch.

Thankfully, Sasha took a seat near the chair, allowing Emma to help the family patriarch.

"You look in good health to me, Mr. Ramsey," she protested honestly enough. Because even though he was thinner than she remembered, he was moving well considering he'd been in an accident that had been the talk of Last Stand for months. "I haven't seen you since the accident, and I'd say you're doing well for a man who had a run-in with a bus."

Everett had been walking to a birthday party the previous spring at a local venue when he was sideswiped by a tourist bus—not hit so much as wrenched around when he'd scrambled out of the way. He'd broken a hip according to what she'd read in the paper, but he'd been lucky since the bus had also collided with a vehicle, killing two young people.

"That's right," Everett said with satisfaction as he successfully plunked into the chair cushions with a huff. "I survived because I'm a tough old coot. Now tell that to my two grandsons, will you?"

Lifting a gnarled finger, the old man pointed behind her. Straightening, she met the green gaze of Wes Ramsey, who was flanked by his older brother, Cal.

Today, while Cal Ramsey looked every inch the cowboy in his boots and jeans, a Stetson shading his face, Wes wore running shorts and a fitted shirt with the name of a workout facility on the front. A pair of discarded earbuds hung around his neck and he breathed like he'd just run a marathon. A bead of sweat trickled down one side of his forehead. And since when did a sweaty man make her feel slightly weak-kneed?

The resemblance between them was strong with their similar features, dark hair, and green eyes. But while they were both good-looking men, it was Wes who captured her attention. He was slightly taller, his build broader, but his appeal had more to do with the way he approached life—serious, determined, and focused. Like if Wes turned his attention to something, he wasn't letting go until it was done. In fact, that's how Wes looked at her right now—as if she was very much his unfinished business.

Heart beating too fast, she tried to cover the fact that she'd stared a bit too long.

"Oh. Um." She swallowed to soothe the throat gone dry and hoped that she didn't seem ridiculously overeager to hang around Wes's family's business while waiting for him to confirm their date. "I'm sure your grandsons recognize your toughness, Mr. Ramsey." Recovering herself, she smiled down at Everett and gave him a wink. "They only need to look in a mirror to see the strength and resilience of the genes you gave them."

Everett laughed while she shifted the placement of the walker so it was off to one side but within reach when he needed it.

"That's true enough," Everett observed, pounding his fist on the arm of the chair. "Stubborn bullheadedness runs in the family." His green eyes—so like his grandsons'—flicked between Emma and Wes before he reached toward Sasha's leash, saying, "Now, why don't you let me visit with this sweet pup here, while you two go catch up? Even old eyes can see you're not just interested in the rutabagas."

Chapter Four

WES'S GRANDFATHER WAS notoriously tough to argue with, and for once, it worked in Wes's favor. When Everett told Emma to leave the dog with him so she could take a walk with Wes, she hesitated for only a moment. But after ensuring her animal's leash was secured to a nearby post, she joined him on the gravel path leading toward the barn.

Wearing a knee-length gray cardigan open over a flouncy blue floral dress, Emma had big shades propped on her head and suede boots on her feet as she came toward him. Her hoop earrings caught the sunlight as she peered back over her shoulder and then met his gaze. He couldn't deny the rush of gladness he'd felt at seeing her outside the farm stand, a feeling that only increased now that he would have her to himself if only for a little while.

Even if her eyes kept darting away from him. Was she nervous?

"I hope I'm not disrupting your day," she began, sounding flustered as she sidestepped a red wagon left out front for young customers to use while their parents shopped. "I didn't think you'd be here."

"So you were trying to avoid me?" He strode past the open pole barns used to store extra farm equipment, still wondering why she seemed jittery.

"No. I just meant that I only came to see the place." She gestured to the weathered wood buildings and the orchards stretching out behind them. "It's been a long time since I visited, and I thought about it more after you mentioned the possibility of your family selling the farm."

The idea of parting with the business had weighed heavily on him in the last months, making the time spent at Rough Hollow bittersweet. He set aside the question of whether or not she was nervous, the old ache of nostalgia for his home returning.

"We were just discussing that." Wes slowed his step near an old flatbed trailer used for hauling fruit, empty now except for some stacked crates. "I was out running one of the orchard paths when Cal flagged me down to help him with Gramp. Everett's convinced he's healthy enough to be on site more, but it makes the staff nervous."

Emma trailed a hand over the fender of an ancient truck parked near the trailer. "Your father won't take a more active role in helping out?"

"And miss the charity golf tournaments with his old baseball buddies?" He couldn't keep the sarcasm from his voice as he leaned a hip onto the flatbed close to the back wheel. A nervous barn swallow swooped out of a nest in the rafters of the open stall, chirping all the way until it disappeared in the trees nearby. "He's always got an excuse, but the bottom line is the same. Dad never liked farm life, and he's too selfish to spend any time here just because it's important to his family."

"What about his father's health? Is he too selfish to spend time with Everett?" Frowning, Emma straightened a fallen stack of bushel baskets on the floor.

Her cutting tone reminded Wes of how much Emma had done to keep her own mother happy, even when the maternal requests were unreasonable. Adeline wanted to drive to the Mexican border just for fun on a school night, even though that meant Emma did her homework in the car and didn't return home until three in the morning. Adeline felt restless at her job and insisted she needed a "summer off," so Emma took full-time office work the summer before senior year. Hell, he even recalled Adeline struggled with tax forms so much she had to pay fines on overdue taxes, an expensive mistake that prompted Emma to undertake the task herself in tenth grade.

No wonder she'd been driven to figure out her dating life sooner rather than later. When Emma saw a problem, she fixed it. Wes had always liked that about her. He understood it, because he felt as if he'd done the same thing. But maybe he'd been selective in which problems he'd chosen to address since he consistently tackled his baseball weaknesses, but he rarely worked on problems around Rough Hollow or with his family.

"Clint figures he fulfilled his duty as a son by being famous so his father could be proud," Wes answered dryly, noticing Emma drifted away from him toward the grassy path between outbuildings. The sun caught her deep auburn hair as she emerged from the overhang. "Would you like to keep walking?"

He straightened from where he'd been leaning against the trailer to join her outside.

She glanced back at him, her blue eyes roaming over him in a decidedly flattering way before she wrenched her head around again.

"I. Um." She nodded even before she spoke. "It would be good to keep moving."

Charging toward the peach trees, Emma rushed so fast her layers of flouncy dress caught a breeze.

And damned if he didn't need to double-time his steps to catch up. When he did, he rewarded himself by capturing her hand.

"Slow down," he urged, determined to know what he was missing. "What's your hurry?"

She swirled around to face him, her lips pursed and her expression a little mutinous. Which made no sense.

Letting go of her hand after the brief contact, he raised his palms to show surrender. "You've been jumpy ever since we started walking," he reminded her, mentally rewinding their conversation. "Did I do anything to make you feel uneasy?"

Emma huffed a sigh. "Uneasy? No." She gestured toward him—head to toe. "But have you forgotten you're a world-class athlete cavorting around in gym shorts and a workout tee like an advertisement for…fitness?" She said it like it was a dirty word. "I think I can count your abs through that shirt."

He smothered a laugh, relieved that he hadn't offended her. And, hell yes, grateful she wasn't immune to him.

"Was I cavorting?" he said, as soberly as he could manage.

"Definitely." She folded her arms across her chest and continued to walk toward the old peach grove. "You already know my dating life has reached an all-time low," she reminded him. "So there's no need to be unfairly attractive."

"Wrong. I'll take any advantage I can get since I only have two weeks to woo you." He planned to make good use of them now that he had a revised understanding of their breakup.

And the more time he spent with Emma, the more time he wanted to spend with her. He hadn't felt that way with any woman since…Emma. He didn't know what it meant for their future, but he wasn't going to ignore the pull of what he felt for her. Especially not when—if left to her own devices—she'd end up with someone all wrong for her, or else packing her bag and moving who knew where.

She was quiet for a long moment, reaching up to touch a low-lying tree branch as they entered the grove. "I still think it's a crazy scheme, and you'll only regret it later when you come to your senses."

"You're already committed. In fact, I was going to call you when I got back from my run to see if you were free tonight."

"Tonight?" She must have forgotten about her determination not to look at him because her blue eyes cut sideways.

"Ty and Alexis are going to barbecue over at the wildflower farm tonight. He invited us to stop by." Wes had been fielding calls from Ty on a regular basis since the guy was tied up in knots over Alexis Harper.

According to Ty, Alexis had kept him at arm's length while she treated him as a patient in her physical therapy practice, but since she'd moved to Last Stand and worked independently, that barrier no longer existed. Even so, the guy couldn't take things out of the friend zone for reasons that were…complicated, to say the least.

"*Us?*" Emma stopped to admire a blue butterfly hovering in the grass. "I'm surprised he knew there was an us."

"You can't blame me for wanting to advertise the good news that you're giving me a chance." Wes didn't reveal the real reason Emma's name came up in a conversation with Ty, unwilling to break the guy's confidence. "And Ty was hoping to have a chance to talk to you."

"To me?" Emma straightened to face him, her cinnamon eyebrows furrowed as her freckled nose wrinkled. "I hardly know him."

Seized with the urge to kiss every freckle—before turning his attention to her very enticing lips—Wes remembered there was a possibility of that kiss tonight. After their date.

"He has his reasons. But either way, I think it could be a good time. Who doesn't like a barbecue and a bonfire?" Not to mention the kissing that would follow.

"I'm game. But you're stacking the odds in your favor by double-dating with my friend, you know," Emma accused softly as she plucked a tall buttercup from the base of a peach tree.

"I plan to pull out all the stops to make sure you enjoy yourself." Spending time with Emma again made him realize how much he wanted her back in his life, for however long he could have her there.

ALEXIS HARPER WIELDED a hoe like a woman possessed, needing an outlet for her nerves. Because although she looked forward to seeing Emma and Wes tonight, she had a whole bunch of mixed feelings about spending more time with Ty Lambert.

She chopped down with the gardening tool to tear a stubborn root, the motion kicking up dirt all over her tennis shoes.

She'd regret her shredded palms the next time she had a patient in her fledgling physical therapy practice, since her hands were frequently called upon to activate muscles. But business was slow as she built her name locally, and her days were too occupied with caring for her ailing father.

Angling the hoe around the canes of a raspberry bush, Alexis dragged the blade toward her through the weedy topsoil. She repeated the action, over and over again, the way she used to do on the farm when she was a teenager and her sister Keely was still at home showing her how to keep the kitchen garden free of weeds.

Some weeks, the food from the garden was all they had, so Alexis had always wanted to do her best to help Keely with the growing. Her mother had been an alcoholic until she ditched her husband and kids one night to run away with her boyfriend. After that, their father had stepped up and moved the family to Last Stand where he'd been born. A move that was good for them all until—a few years later—loneliness had eaten away at their father and he'd returned to drinking too. That's when things had gotten tough for the Harper sisters. But Keely had shouldered the brunt of the work, ensuring the house was clean and Alexis ate.

Back then, if Alexis didn't do a good job hoeing the garden, Keely would pick up the slack. The knowledge that Alexis hadn't pulled her own weight had bugged her later in life, especially when she'd only been able to attend university thanks to Keely's money management and sacrifices. She owed her sister, no matter what Keely said. And Alexis refused to let Windy Meadows Wildflowers go out of business now that Keely was finally exploring the world outside of Last Stand.

A man's voice at the edge of the lawn called her from her thoughts.

"Alexis?" Ty Lambert strode toward her, all six-foot-four, muscle-clad inches of him. His dark brown hair brushed his collar now, though he buzzed it short during baseball season.

"Let me give you a hand."

She'd met him when she'd been his physical therapist during a rehab stint last year, and she still felt a little amazed that of all the women he met in his career—and she knew it was a hefty number—that he seemed to want to be with her. Trust came hard for her with anyone after being a witness to the implosion of her parents' marriage. And trusting Ty would be especially tough considering his life on the road, surrounded by appreciative female fans. Plus, there was the added concern that Ty shared an old, unhealthy habit with Alexis that she needed to break. Her thrill-seeking days were behind her, while the whole reason she'd met Ty through her physical therapy work was to rehab his broken body after a motorcycle accident.

She understood his demons a little too well since she'd nearly died in a hang-gliding accident brought on by her own risk-taking. She'd committed to Al-Anon in the last two years to become more aware of her stressors and how it related to her family, but she needed to be vigilant.

And her life felt so full of stress right now, she found it tough to scavenge enough energy to be careful around a man who seriously attracted her.

"That's not necessary." She guessed time had gotten away from her if Ty was already here. She'd suggested a barbecue on the farm with friends in an ongoing effort to keep things light between them in spite of the mutual attraction. "I should shower and change before Emma and Wes arrive. But if you don't mind helping out, the bonfire pit still needs to be prepped."

Stopping next to her, Ty took the hoe from her hands. She tried not to wince as she released her grip, even that movement causing a sting in her torn palms.

"Are you okay?" He must have noticed her slight flinch, staring down at her with a concerned expression in his blue green eyes. "Did you get a splinter?"

He studied her with a focus that any woman would find flattering, and he was always attentive like that, focusing on *her* and not just the attraction between them. Dressed in jeans and boots with a pale blue button-down, Ty smelled like sandalwood and pine, so good that she wanted to lean closer to breathe him in. Except that she shouldn't when she wasn't sure where things were heading between them.

His baseball season would take him away for spring training and then a minimum of one hundred and sixty-two games, which meant she'd hardly see him from the middle of February to the end of September. Longer if his team went to the postseason. Who could build a relationship around a schedule like that? Especially when she was committed to being with her father through his last days? The ache in her chest deepened every time she thought of it.

"No." She tucked her hands to her sides before he could take one of them. Even when she'd been Ty's physical therapist, touching him had cut right through her professional reserve. Now—months after she'd quit her job for his team and opened her own practice—she couldn't use the excuse of her work as a barrier for the attraction anymore. "I just got a few blisters. They'll be fine once I put some ointment on them."

He frowned down at her. "Why didn't you call me? I would have been glad to help."

"And risk your hands when you've got to swing a bat two weeks from now?" She sidled past all his delectable male strength and waved him to follow her toward the house. "Let me show you where the wood is stacked for the bonfire and you can decide how much we need. The weeding isn't urgent anyway."

She kept moving, feeling like the only way she could get through her days was by barreling through.

"You work too hard," he accused gently, echoing a sentiment she'd heard in her latest phone call with her sister. Ty had never disguised his tendency to be blunt. "Half the reason I accepted Wes's invitation to stay at the Ramsey place this month is so that I could see you more often. If I can lighten your load, Alexis, I wish you'd let me help."

Something twisted in her chest at the idea that he was in town for her—at least partly. She knew he came back to oversee the expansion of the baseball camp that Nate Ramsey had started last summer, but she'd known he wanted to see her more often. To take their relationship from a flirtatious friendship to more.

And she was scared to take that step for so many reasons.

Stopping near the stone fire pit behind the house, Alexis leaned on one of the big wooden chairs surrounding it. She was fully aware she was putting physical barriers between her and Ty. She needed them more and more often, to keep her hands to herself.

"That's kind of you." She was glad that they'd invited Emma and Wes tonight. She'd need the distraction. "But I wouldn't know what to do with myself if I wasn't working hard. Besides, Keely managed the farm and took care of Dad for years while I was in school and then working for the Houston Stars. I'm glad to be able to repay her sacrifice in some small way."

Ty regarded her skeptically, tilting his head to one side to study her. "Would Keely be glad to know how much time you're devoting to Windy Meadows Wildflowers instead of your physical therapy practice?"

No. Keely would be furious. But Alexis needed outlets for her stress caring for their father. Not that she minded the time. If anything, what upset her most was knowing he had so little time left. Every day his skin seemed a little grayer, his body shutting down after too much damage to his liver over the years. He wasn't eligible to be on the transplant list.

The weight of that knowledge—that he was dying—made her contemplate skydiving. Bungee jumping. Free climbing a ninety-degree rock face. Anything to get out of her own head. Compared to those things, starting something with Ty Lambert seemed like a safer bet. Or was she justifying how much she wanted to be with him?

"Maybe not, but I can't help wanting to do what I can to keep her business going while she's on the road with Nate. But the next time I want to work hard, I promise I'll call you to help me," she assured him, needing to extricate herself from the conversation and his too-tempting presence before she did something unwise. Like kissing him until they were both breathless. "For now, I'd better clean up before Emma and Wes arrive. The woodpile is under a tarp behind the shed if you want to fill the fire pit."

Ty nodded as he propped the hoe against a chair back and stepped closer to her. "Of course. But I hope we can continue this conversation after the other guests leave tonight."

His eyes fixed on hers, and she felt sucked into the heat of that intense gaze, her nerve endings hyper aware as he reached up to stroke a long strand of hair from her forehead.

A shiver swept through her. Her throat went dry.

Her heart might worry about things heating up with Ty, but her body seemed very in favor of the idea.

"I—I'm not sure," she murmured finally, her gaze switching channels between his lips and his eyes. Back and forth.

Maybe he noticed, because one side of his mouth kicked up in a smile.

"I'm just asking to talk to you," he reminded her, tucking her loose hair back where it belonged and inciting another whole-body shiver with that featherlight touch. "That's all."

Right. Because "just talking" never led to heated kisses and passionate embraces.

Or more.

Still, she couldn't deny that she was curious. What if kissing Ty could be a more limited risk-taking experience? A thrill that would have set parameters and came with an expiration date in the form of spring training.

With a jerky nod, she agreed. "We'll talk later."

The flare of heat in his sea-green eyes almost made her forget what she was doing. She stared into them for a long moment before she remembered that she needed to get ready for company.

Spinning on her heel, she took her torn-up palms and her wary heart, and headed indoors.

Chapter Five

WARMED BY THE flames of the bonfire later that evening, Emma sat on the edge of her seat so she could monitor the progress of a marshmallow on the end of her stick. The barbecue meal with Ty, Alexis, and Wes had been fun and casual, making her date night low-pressure in a way she appreciated. Although now, as the four of them prepared their own s'mores for dessert, Emma noticed Wes's gaze linger on her every now and then in a way that warmed her more than the flames.

Keeping her focus on the correct distance between her marshmallow and the coals beneath, Emma listened while Ty regaled them with a story about his rookie season from his seat on the opposite side of the fire pit. If she watched what she was doing, she couldn't accidentally meet Wes's eyes as he studied her from his seat beside her. Because as much as Wes might say he wanted a second chance with her, she still wasn't sure what that meant in his mind.

And she refused to have her heart broken by the same man twice.

Although she couldn't deny the thought of kissing him again had consumed her thoughts ever since their talk by

Hickory Creek. Surely she could indulge in that much without putting her heart at risk?

A hiss and flare at the end of her stick made her realize she'd dipped the long, skinny branch too close to the conflagration. She'd managed to keep her thoughts away from Wes for all of two seconds.

Bringing the flaming treat closer, she blew out the charred dessert and reached for a graham cracker from the plate balanced on the arm of her wooden chair. The fire popped and crackled, sending a few sparks onto the stones at Emma's feet.

"Here. Let me help," Wes offered lifting the plate to bring it closer to her just in time for the melting confection to slide off the stick and onto the chocolate square. "Perfect timing."

He capped the top of the marshmallow with another graham cracker before passing her the plate. Alexis spoke up from her seat on Emma's other side.

"I have a question for the guys," she started, wrapping the tail of her long blond ponytail around her hand. She must have already eaten her dessert because she leaned back in her chair. "What do you look forward to most about spring training?"

Wes shook his head and pointed to Ty. "He's done this more times than me. Ty, what do you like about it?"

On the opposite side of the fire pit, Ty took his time, double-stacking his marshmallows on a cracker as he spoke. "It's the great equalizer in baseball. In spring, there's no difference between the guy who earns mega bucks and the twenty-year-old rookie trying to earn his spot. We all do wind sprints and base running drills. We all ride a bus in uniform just like we did in our high school days. It's more fun and less pressure."

Wes laughed. "I don't think the rookie would agree with you. The pressure is on for the guys trying to earn a spot."

"But the experience of playing ball is so much different in the spring," Ty insisted as he set aside his toasting stick, leaning it up against the vacant chair beside him. "Fans aren't going to heckle the new guy if he messes up a play. The stakes are low for the games. Winning isn't everything."

Emma glanced sideways to see Wes's expression, curious if he agreed with his friend's assessment since Wes had always put a tremendous amount of pressure on himself where baseball was concerned.

"Dad has some good stories from his spring training days," Wes admitted. He skimmed a rock along the dirt with the toe of his boot, his gaze following the progress of the stone. "My father is a consummate BS artist about a lot of things, but I know most of his stories from his spring training days are true since I've gotten to meet a lot of the guys he played with over the years. It seems like those low-key times together as a team did more to create lasting bonds than whatever happened the rest of the season."

Emma was surprised at the hint of wistfulness in Wes's voice, something she'd never recalled from him before when he spoke of his father. Then again, maybe the sense of nostalgia had more to do with what Wes liked about baseball than his dad. She wanted to believe that, after all his hard work and sacrifice to get on a major league team, he would find something in it to enjoy.

Alexis popped out of her seat to retrieve the tray of s'mores ingredients and carried it around the fire pit circle like a dutiful hostess. "Keely is going to Mesa, Arizona, with Nate when he heads to spring training with his team."

Emma shouldn't be surprised. She hadn't spoken to Keely much since Christmas, but she knew Alexis's sister was enjoying life in Chicago with Nate Ramsey. Nate had been traded last summer, and Keely had packed her bags to be with him after much lobbying by Alexis to go chase her dreams outside of Last Stand for a while.

Wes shook his head as Alexis offered the tray, leaning back in his chair with a frown. "Dad has already rented a house in Arizona for the spring, halfway between Mesa and Scottsdale, so he can attend as many games as possible to see Nate, Cal, and me."

Any hint of affection she might have heard in his voice before was gone. Emma knew his father's presence at his games added another level of pressure to a time in his life that already came with heavy expectations.

Before she could weigh the wisdom of the impulse, she reached over to Wes's chair and laid a comforting hand on his arm.

"At least I have the option of deciding whether or not I want to spend spring break with my mom," she offered, empathizing with him. "She invited me out to Beverly Hills for the week, but when I tried to explain the flights were too astronomical for that week, she said I should just get in the car and drive." The conversation had brought back all the old tension and stress of life with Adeline. "As if it would be fun to spend half of my days off behind the wheel. I told myself then and there that I needed to start building a life with roots so deep she couldn't suggest I tear them all up to join her wherever she happens to be."

Wes's gaze missed nothing as he studied her from the next seat over. Awareness pinged through her between the eye contact and the way her fingers rested on his strong forearm, so she withdrew her hand. But the warmth coursing through her didn't ease.

"I hope that's not the deeper cause for rushing your romantic life," Wes said in a low voice so that only she could hear him. "You don't need a family to shield you from your mom."

The heat she'd been feeling chilled, indignation taking its place.

"I've been handling Adeline for a lot of years," she reminded him, straightening in her seat.

"I realize that. I only meant that you can refuse to jump when she calls you even without a family for an excuse."

"I don't *jump* for her at any time." She bristled. Unlike him, she didn't bother to lower her voice. "Don't judge me."

Alexis and Ty looked at her with surprised expressions, but Emma couldn't be bothered to explain. Unable to stay in her seat, she rose to her feet and grabbed the tray full of leftover food that Alexis had just finished passing around.

"I'll take this inside for you." Emma seized on the first excuse to escape. To cool off.

She marched toward the Harper farmhouse, funneling her anger into the stomp of her feet through the patchy grass. She was almost at the stairs into the back door of the kitchen when a broad male arm reached over her head to open it for her.

Ty stood just behind her. "Here you go. I'll give you a hand."

"Thank you," she murmured, telling herself she had no reason to feel embarrassed. She hadn't presumed to tell Wes how to live *his* life.

Emma stepped up into the kitchen, depositing the tray on the butcher-block countertop near the sink. She knew the Harper home well enough, having visited Keely here plenty of times in her teens. Plus, Emma had helped Alexis bring the food outside at the start of their barbecue, so she remembered roughly where things were stored in the cabinets.

Too agitated to make polite conversation with Ty, she proceeded to open cupboard doors and return items to their proper homes.

"If you're here to make excuses for Wes—" she began when Ty remained quiet for a long moment.

"Heck no." Ty shook his head and paced the kitchen floor, stopping behind a ladder-back chair at the table. "Nothing like that. I realize my timing isn't the best, but I had a favor I wanted to ask."

Closing the pantry door, Emma was surprised that he sounded so serious, even though she recalled Wes saying that Ty had hoped to speak to her tonight. She didn't know Ty well, but from what she'd seen of him so far, he struck her as a happy-go-lucky guy. She remembered he'd missed most of the last baseball season because of a motorcycle accident, and that his team had wanted him to rein in his risk-taking behaviors. Keely had been worried about Alexis seeing so much of Ty since Alexis had a thrill-seeking streak of her own.

"I'll help if I can," Emma replied, relieved to talk about something besides her dating life. Or Wes.

She ventured closer to the kitchen table where a gingham-print tablecloth added a cheerful note to the worn finishes of the place. The Harper farmhouse hadn't been renovated in many years, but it was lovingly cared for by Keely and Alexis. Their invalid father had been asleep—or at least in his room—ever since Emma had arrived.

Ty looked up at her now, his blue-green eyes steady. "I didn't realize you were an educator until that night when Wes and I ran into you at the Last Stand Saloon. An English teacher."

Of all the things she imagined a famous baseball player might say to her, this hadn't been on the list.

She nodded. "I am. I instruct ninth graders at Creekbend High School."

"What I'm going to tell you—" He hesitated and then

heaved out a harsh sigh. "I wish you'd keep it in confidence even if you can't help me."

She couldn't miss the strain in his voice. The worry. He wasn't that much older than her or Alexis, and yet fine lines fanned out from his eyes as he looked at her, as if the secret had weighed on him for a long time.

"You have my word," she promised, wondering what was on his mind to make him so upset.

"I haven't told Alexis yet," he clarified, and she realized he was asking her to keep a secret from her closest friend in Last Stand.

She didn't like it, but she nodded.

Releasing the back of the chair, he stood tall as he spoke. "I'm a functional illiterate," he announced, speaking the word with distaste. "And I wondered if you could help me learn to read."

Stunned, Emma blinked up at him. How could an elite athlete have made it through high school *and* a competitive college without knowing how to read and write? Or at least, without knowing how to read and write *well*?

And yet, she knew firsthand that it happened. She saw kids moved through the grades all the time who hadn't learned the material necessary to be promoted. For that matter, skilled athletes were in such high demand that they could sometimes—depending on the school—barely attend classes so they could focus on their sport. As long as their tutors provided notes and grades, the normal educational parameters didn't apply.

"Ty, I'm so sorry you didn't get the education you deserved." She couldn't imagine how hard it had been for him to ask for her help, and she didn't want to discourage him. "There are better resources than I would be, however—"

His broad shoulders fell. "Emma, you have no idea how tough it was for me to ask you this—"

"Okay," she agreed quickly, wanting to make it clear that she would help him. But she also needed him to know he had other options. "I will absolutely work with you, Ty, if you want me to. I just wanted to point out that there are really good programs specifically designed for this. Online programs, even, where you can work anonymously and at your own pace."

"And what if I read the directions wrong?" he said bitterly, his hands flexing at his sides. "I could accidentally delete my account, or publish my second-grade-level essay to the internet."

Frustration practically steamed off the words, making her understand his point.

"I'll help you," she promised, even though she knew it would be difficult once he left Last Stand to attend spring training. "We'll have to come up with a work schedule. Do you have time to meet this week?"

Outside the kitchen, she heard Alexis's laughter and remembered that it was going to be tricky keeping the arrangement a secret from her friend.

"Name the place and I'll be there." Ty spoke with an earnestness that boded well for their future efforts together, although she knew it could be incredibly frustrating for adults to work at the remedial pace needed to learn reading later in life. "And thank you, Emma. You have no idea how much it means that you're going to help me." His attention shifted to a window overlooking the bonfire in the backyard. "I won't feel right trying to win a place in Alexis's life until I'm worthy of her."

Emma wanted to argue that the school system's failure to teach him didn't make him unworthy in any way, but the sound of Wes's voice outside the kitchen warned her that the others were about to join them.

"Why don't you meet me at Creekbend after the kids get out of class on Monday?" she said hurriedly instead.

As Ty nodded, the back door opened, and Alexis stepped into the kitchen followed by Wes.

Wes's eyes settled on her, reminding her of his earlier presumption.

"Are you ready to head home?" he asked.

An unwanted shiver of awareness tickled her senses despite her annoyance. He'd driven them both to the Harper house, so going home meant being alone with him again.

Nodding, Emma began to say her good nights to their friends, all the while wondering how she could still crave a kiss from a man who riled her the way Wes did. Although maybe a part of the appeal was in remembering that he'd brought her here tonight for his friend's sake, knowing she'd keep Ty's confidence. Knowing she'd help.

Some of her anger subsided as her perspective shifted.

Wes Ramsey might get under her skin, but clearly Ty put a lot of faith in Wes's friendship and discretion to have entrusted his secret to him.

When they walked alone together across the front lawn to his pickup truck, Emma could feel all the old feelings for him crowding her chest, mingling with some new ones. Heart beating fast, she stepped up the running board and into the passenger seat before buckling her seat belt.

Every nerve ending flickered to life as he opened the driver's side door and took the seat beside her.

WES HAD MADE a mistake in spouting off to Emma. He recognized it as soon as the words had left his mouth. Putting the pickup into gear as they left the Harper farm, he thought through how to apologize since he wouldn't make the mistake of letting hasty words fly twice in the same evening.

It seemed strange to him that it happened in the first place. Of all the Ramsey brothers, he was the quietest. The one most likely to keep his own counsel. Yet with Emma, sometimes his thoughts flowed unchecked. Was it because there'd been a time in his life where he'd shared so much with her? She'd been one of the few people in his life that he'd let get close to him.

Which was why he'd trusted her to help Ty.

He took Laurel Street north, passing the high school and

leaving Hickory Creek behind them before he spoke.

"I was out of line tonight, and I apologize." He figured he'd start there since it needed to be said. He wasn't ready to venture his guess about *why* he'd felt comfortable enough with her to say something without thinking it through first, though. But he hazarded a guess on where the thought had come from as he continued. "Having been manipulated by my dad often enough, I was probably speaking from my own shadows when I said you didn't need a shield from your mom. That doesn't excuse it, of course. I should handle my own business before I make suggestions to anyone else about theirs."

"Thank you for acknowledging that." She turned toward him on the bench seat, her denim-clad knee still not close enough to him in the full-sized pickup. "I know from the outside it seems like I'm rushing things, but that's only because I don't like to waste time once I know what I want."

He wanted to ask her more about that, but he also didn't want to rile her more when he still owed her his thanks for what she'd done tonight. His gaze snagged on her as he turned onto Wisteria Lane and headed farther from the town's center. She looked too damned good with her eclectic mix of clothing—a flannel shirt tied around her waist and a chunky knit sweater opened over an army-green T-shirt. Her red ankle boots were a favorite of hers that he remembered from her college days. A butterfly comb on one side of her auburn hair revealed her delicate features and tempting lips.

"You've always been decisive," he acknowledged. "And I

appreciate you helping Ty even though you had every reason to be upset with me." He cracked his window to let in the fresh night air, hoping to keep his wits about him in spite of the hint of ginger and grapefruit in the air, scents he'd always associate with the essential oils she used on her skin instead of perfume.

"He told you that I agreed to work with him?" She sounded surprised.

Pulling into the driveway of her cottage on the edge of town, Wes switched off the truck lights and put the vehicle in park. Hidden white spotlights in the garden shone around the front patio pointed at the house, ensuring her front door and walkway were visible even after sunset. She'd done a lot with the place since she'd lived there with her mother. Though small, the cottage was freshly painted and well-tended, reflecting Emma's pleasure in having a home to call her own.

"Ty didn't need to tell me." Wes glanced across the cab at her. She hadn't changed so much in the last few years that he would have misjudged her giving nature. "If I hadn't been certain you'd help him, I wouldn't have let him put himself on the line by asking you in the first place. It's tough for him to talk about it."

"I wish he wouldn't hide the problem from Alexis. It's not his fault the school system failed him." She frowned as she smoothed and toyed with the loose sleeves of the flannel shirt still tied about her waist. "I can't imagine how stressful it must be to go through life trying to compensate for something like that."

"Me either. You would think he had the world by the tail with the money he makes and the career he's had in baseball." Wes envied his stats. But he knew firsthand how much trouble Ty took to hide his illiteracy from the world. "Yet he'd trade it in a minute for being able to read."

"Do you really think so?" She stopped the restless weaving of the flannel shirtsleeves together, her blue gaze steady.

His blood heated, remembering the kiss he still craved from her tonight.

"I know so." Wes had been in Last Stand with his brother Nate and Ty at the end of the previous baseball season when Ty had said as much. "How long do you think it will take to teach him?"

She shook her head, the butterfly clip reflecting the landscape lights as she moved. "It's impossible to say. If he's motivated and doesn't have a learning disability, the work can move quickly. But it can be frustrating for adult learners to tackle material they've wrestled with in the past."

He nodded, taking in what she'd said. The thought of a learning disability never occurred to him, and he wondered if Ty had ever explored the possibility. Wes remembered well how much emphasis was placed on sports in his own scholastic career. If Ty had been in a similar environment, testing for learning issues might have been overlooked in favor of keeping him on track with his training.

"Thank you for helping him, Emma." He reached across the cab to squeeze her hand briefly, needing to acknowledge her kindness to his friend even if she wasn't happy with him tonight. "Let me at least walk you to the door."

Exiting the truck, he strode around the cargo bed to open the passenger door, but she was already on her feet in the driveway when he reached her side. He accompanied her up the front steps, doing his damnedest not to follow the sway of her hips with his eyes and failing. Once they stood on the cottage's planked porch, he wanted to pull her into his arms for that good-night kiss they'd talked about. But the need to feel her in his arms was tempered by caution. He was playing the long game here, looking well beyond the short term when it came to Emma.

"I hope I haven't ruined my chances of a second date." He stopped short of the bright welcome mat, turning to face her in the porch light. "I was looking forward to seeing you more over the next two weeks."

Although it was technically less than that now. The thought twisted his gut as he watched her rock back on the heels of her red boots.

She looked down at her feet for a moment, her long lashes fanning over her cheeks before she met his gaze. "I'm willing to try again if you are."

Relief coursed through him, and he released a pent-up breath.

"Good. That's…good." He told himself to say good night and thank his lucky stars for the victory, but his feet stayed rooted to the spot. To keep himself from staring at her, he shifted his gaze to the house behind her. "You've fixed the place up. It looks great."

She'd lived here when they'd dated. Her mom renting the house from a retired rancher, Angus Richards, who lived in the next town over. Back then, the place had been falling down around their ears. But the windows were new and so was the front door. Everything looked freshly painted.

"I've been slowly fixing it up," she admitted peering back over her shoulder.

"Did Angus finally decide to sell?" Wes asked, wondering if his grandfather would be following suit soon. The idea of Rough Hollow going to someone else didn't feel right to Wes.

"No." Emma shook her head. "I still rent, but he doesn't mind if I paint. And he reimbursed me for the price of the door. I installed it myself."

"I'm impressed. I'm sure your landlord is only too happy to have someone working to keep up the place." His attention shifted to the new shutters, and he remembered showing up at her window before, the past mingling with the present. "Do you remember when I dropped you off here after our first date?"

One side of her lips curved. Her dimple flashed. "When Adeline tried to coax you inside by offering you a beer?"

Wes was relieved she could smile about it now. "You were so mad at her."

Emma reached for the sleeves of the flannel tied around her waist, winding the sleeves around each other. "Mom always liked to be the center of attention, even with my friends. Plus, I was angry she ruined the end of my date when I should have been getting my good-night kiss."

His heart thumped harder in his chest at the memory.

"But I came back an hour later." He'd driven halfway home before circling back. He'd parked his truck up the road and then walked onto her property, hoping he'd picked out the right room as hers. "I just thought I'd throw a pebble at your window, so I'd be the last person you saw before you went to sleep that night."

He'd kept to the shadows at the edge of the lawn. Until she'd opened the sash and called out to him.

Her dimple deepened. "Except I didn't let you off the hook once I saw you between the trees."

The memory was one of the sweetest he had with this woman. And it rolled right through him now, conjuring up her taste. Her scent. All his hopes about her.

He reached for her hands and linked their fingers. The breeze lifted her hair from her face and then ruffled it against her cheek. He got lost in the deep blue of her eyes.

"I kissed you then," he reminded her, wanting her to remember it as vividly as he always did.

She edged closer to him, a hint of her fragrance teasing his nose.

"I wanted you to," she said softly, her voice a breathless caress against his lips.

For a moment, he let the wanting fill him up. Remind him that Emma Garcia was special. Important.

And then, once he trusted that he understood how much rode on this kiss, he lowered his mouth over hers to claim it once more.

Chapter Six

EMMA'S WHOLE WORLD narrowed to that kiss.

Her heartbeat galloped from it. Her skin warmed in spite of the cool night air. Lips tingling from the light contact of his, she felt awareness rise inside her as sweet and effervescent as champagne bubbles in a glass. Wes's hands cupped her shoulders, steadying her for the gentle slide of his lips along hers. Testing. Exploring.

The scent of the bonfire rose from his clothes and skin. He tasted like marshmallow. Emma gripped the open placket of his flannel shirt, her fingers flexing into the soft nape even as she told herself to ease away from him. To break the contact that mesmerized her.

She'd kissed Wes hundreds of times while they were dating, and yet the feelings this moment inspired felt all new. Maybe because they weren't the same people anymore.

With that reminder—and all the good and bad things that came with it—her fingers flexed against his chest. She was about to pull back when he eased away first. Regret whispered through her that she couldn't go on kissing him for days on end.

For a moment, she blinked up at him, trying to gather

her bearings.

"I should say good night." His words breathed over her still-damp mouth.

With an effort, she relinquished her hold on his shirt.

"Right," she agreed with a jerky nod, knowing she should go but unable to pull her gaze from his. "Good night, Wes."

For a long moment, she stared up into his green eyes turned shades of gray in the dim light of the porch. If a kiss undid her this way, what would happen if she fell for Wes all over again?

The thought rattled her, finally forcing her to turn away from him and fit her key in the front door lock. Tonight, at least, her heart was still intact. She'd just have to be careful to keep it that way.

❧

EMMA THREW HERSELF into teaching to keep from spending too much time thinking about Wes Ramsey.

Her students always filled her days, but now that she'd taken on Ty Lambert as an adult learning pupil, her work lingered into the evenings. For the first four days of the school week, she'd met Ty at Creekbend to introduce him to a reading program and acclimate him to the online tools he could use in his off-hours to help with his alphabetics, fluency, and vocabulary. Once he'd understood the visual cues on the computer program so that he felt confident navigating it alone, Ty had immersed himself in the educational tool, knocking out one exercise after another in his free time so that their one-on-one time could be spent on areas where he'd struggled.

Now, as she prepared to meet Ty for their fifth teaching session late Friday afternoon, she drove out of the parking lot at Creekbend High School and headed south on Pecan Street toward the old Ramsey farmhouse. Windows rolled down in her crossover model SUV, Emma couldn't deny a flare of anticipation at the possibility of seeing Wes there. Emma had asked Ty if they could meet somewhere besides the school today since the cleaning staff appreciated having the building emptied out as early as possible on a Friday. Ty had suggested the Rough Hollow property—the house, not the farm store—since Ty had a workout scheduled with Wes before the teaching session.

Wes. The man whose kiss was the last thing she thought about every night before she fell asleep. He'd called her midweek to see if she was free for dinner, but she'd demurred for reasons she hadn't quite picked through. She'd told him that Ty's lessons were taking up a lot of her time, and that was true. But her bigger concern was that she hadn't figured out how to steel herself against the possibility of falling for Wes all over again. And until she had a plan, how could she afford to meet him—and kiss him—again?

Now, Emma slowed her vehicle as she got behind a farm tractor close to Rough Hollow. The purple-winged fairy hanging from her rearview mirror swung in time to her braking. Texas redbuds were in bloom on either side of the road as the number of houses thinned out. Golden coreopsis and pink primroses danced in the breeze as she turned down the gravel driveway toward the historic Ramsey homestead. Everett lived in the original home, while the larger farmhouse on the next lot over had traditionally gone to the oldest Ramsey son and his family.

Wes had grown up in that farmhouse with his brothers and their younger sister, Lara, who'd left Last Stand the day she turned eighteen. Their father had briefly relocated his family to a tacky mansion on the other side of town, but their mother had left that house once she'd discovered her husband's infidelity. These days, Wes's mom maintained the old Ramsey farmhouse while Clint and his second wife kept the ugly monstrosity that Clint had built. Emma had always found a lot to admire about Hailey Decker, a woman who'd been given short shrift in her marriage but still kept a good relationship with her former father-in-law. A woman who'd invested Clint's baseball earnings wisely and spent her half on charitable projects.

Emma's car jostled over a bump in the horseshoe driveway and continued toward the detached, two-story double garage in back of the main farmhouse. The structure was painted white with black shutters to match the nearby home. But her attention wasn't on the building.

Because as the back lawn came into view, Emma could see both Ty and Wes. Side by side, the friends sprinted across the yard. Dressed in running shorts and sleeveless tees that showed off their muscles, they tore over the grass. Knees churning, elbows driving, they charged so hard and fast that they had to pull up short before plowing headlong into Hailey Decker's vegetable patch ringed by marigolds.

And *wow*.

Emma nearly rolled into the back of Wes's pickup truck, she was so distracted by the sight of so much…maleness. Abruptly jamming her foot on the brake, gravel spewing from under the tires as she blinked fast then parked the car, willing herself not to stare. And although both men were equally well built, it was always Wes who captured her full attention. Wes who populated her idle thoughts and showed up in her dreams at night, even though she told herself not to let him in.

"Emma," he called to her now from the far end of the lawn as she got out of her car.

Even from thirty yards away she could see the ridges of muscle in his arms and thighs. She had to unstick her tongue from the roof of her mouth since her throat had gone dry.

"Hi," she managed to croak before she recovered herself, smoothing the front of the simple blue kimono she wore over her sweater like a blazer.

The action helped her to keep her resolve to not look at the man's thighs under any circumstances.

"I'm sorry we ran late," Ty offered jogging past her to pick up some workout equipment on the lawn—a few cones, and a couple of agility ladders. "I can shower in five minutes and be ready to work."

"No need to rush," Emma assured him, remaining on the gravel path that flanked the circular lawn in the hope she wouldn't get too close to Wes when the sight of him affected her this way.

But Wes strode toward her like a man with a sense of purpose, his trainers light on the grass as he moved with athletic ease. Her gaze swept across the gray cotton of his shirt, taking in the way his pectoral muscles stretched the fabric. She'd seen plenty of baseball players who didn't invest a lot of effort in their training since the sport was not as physically demanding as some others like football or hockey. But Wes looked ready to compete in most anything and win, his fitness level obvious.

"Ty, I'll put things away," Wes told his friend, clamping a restraining hand on Ty's shoulder. "Cal might want to work out later anyhow."

"Sure thing. Thanks, man." Straightening, Ty jogged toward the exterior staircase leading up to the second story of the garage where Emma happened to know there was a furnished apartment.

She knew that because she and Wes had sneaked in there a few times to be together during the summer after their freshman year of college. She'd lost her virginity in the bedroom up there, one of the few times in her life she'd done something simply because she wanted to even though she hadn't been certain their relationship would last. Even when she hadn't trusted him with her future, she'd trusted him with that all-important first time, and she'd never regretted that. He'd been so thoughtful with her body. Like everything else Wes chose to do in life, he did it very, very well. Memories bombarded her from all sides so that it felt disorienting to her when Wes spoke again.

"Ty says he's learning a lot from you," he observed, hauling her attention away from the building. "It sounds like it's going well."

Emma tried to refocus as she watched Wes return the agility ladders to their original spots on the grass, the equipment helpful for footwork drills, she remembered. She'd excelled in softball as a girl, but she'd played a few seasons of basketball too, and her coaches had used the training equipment a few times.

"Ty is committed and smart," she murmured, unwilling to take credit for the efforts he was making on his own. "I think he just needed someone to introduce him to the right tools."

She was happy to work with him, but it worried her that he hadn't been honest with Alexis about how he was spending a large portion of his time. Alexis had been busy with her father's health problems over the past week, so she hadn't asked Emma to get together recently. But she'd texted twice and mentioned that she hadn't seen Ty since the barbecue. Emma guessed that was because of the long hours he was putting into the program she'd shared with him. Plus, it was inevitable she'd see her friend soon, and then how would she avoid the topic of Ty?

"You've done more than that, Emma. Have a seat while

you're waiting for him." Wes gestured toward an open shed that had been converted into an entertaining area, complete with dining table, fan, and bar. Lots of quirky accents decorated the space, including an old truck fender and a tall rooster sculpture with chipped paint.

There were numerous outbuildings around the property that used to be a working ranch. Now, peach trees stretched in every direction beyond the vegetable garden and yard.

"Thanks." She stepped out of the sun and into the shade of the pole barn, taking a seat at the end of the walnut table and dropping her bag into the chair beside her. "Don't let me keep you."

Wes strode past her toward the small bar against the back wall. He opened the door of an old refrigerator and withdrew a glass pitcher of water.

"Seriously? There's nowhere I'd rather be right now than talking to you, Emma Garcia. I know you were hiding from me this week." He pulled two glasses from a lower cabinet and filled them both from the water pitcher.

"Hardly," she retorted, digging in her bag for a comb to fasten one side of her hair that tickled her cheek thanks to a mild breeze. "I've been busy, and I know you have been too. Have you and Cal figured out a plan for Rough Hollow?"

She withdrew a hair clip covered with red silk roses slid it in place while Wes carried over the drinks and took a seat at the table across from her. He passed her a glass of water on a wooden coaster in the shape of Texas.

"Not yet, but don't deflect." His green eyes fixed on her

as the overhead fan cast slow-moving shadows across his face. "I wanted to find a time to see you this week and you came up with excuses for anything I suggested. I didn't call you on it then because I was afraid you'd retreat completely. But now that I only have one more week in town, I can't afford to just hope you'll change your mind."

Outside, a bird chirped cheerfully from a nearby perch as Emma weighed her options. Delaying seeing Wes hadn't exactly shored up her defenses to keep from falling for him again even though he was slated to leave town soon. If anything, she felt more vulnerable to his directness and his physical appeal than ever. It didn't help that they were having this conversation so close to a space that held a lot of fond memories from their shared past.

"I'm worried about what will happen when you leave town," she admitted, knowing it revealed far too much about her feelings. "The kiss reminded me how fast things could escalate between us, and I'm not sure I'm ready for...that."

He lowered his glass, a thoughtful look settling along his dark eyebrows. "Meaning you're concerned about increased intimacy? Or the lack of a plan for a continued relationship once I start spring training?"

The hum of awareness that buzzed just beneath her skin vibrated with new urgency.

"Both." Glancing down, she traced a line of the dark wood grain in the table when she would far rather be tracing the lines of Wes's muscles. Or his mouth. "That is, I'm not sure how I feel about either one. Or about the possibility of saying goodbye at the end of the week."

In an instant he was on his feet and around to her side of the table, pulling an unused chair with him so he could sit very close to her. His thighs bracketed hers, his bare knee grazing the denim seam of her jeans.

"All the more reason we need to talk."

Her gaze darted to his, her body firing with awareness of his proximity. His warmth. The scent of his skin tugged her focus away from his words so that she had to answer slowly, replaying what he'd said.

"I might be..." She bit her lip against the urge to lean forward and taste him. "That is, I'm conversationally challenged when we're this close."

Her heart thudded harder.

She watched his pupils dilate. Heard his sharp intake of breath as her awareness set fire to his. She'd been with him before, so Emma knew the signs. And it took all her willpower not to act on them.

"So we go out on a date." He nodded slowly, as if he'd come to a decision. His thighs on either side of hers blocked the breeze, making the air more still between them. "Surround ourselves with people. Put a table and a couple of plates between us to ensure a conversation happens."

A thrill shot through her before panic followed in its wake. The more time she spent with Wes, the more she craved exploring the attraction. And that still scared her because he could do far more damage to her heart than anyone of the other so-called matches on her prospective dating list.

"We had a table between us a minute ago," she reminded him, tipping her head to indicate the wooden surface where her water glass rested. "And look where we ended up."

"Close enough to kiss." His hand lifted to her hair, stroking a lock between thumb and forefinger. "But I won't let that happen until we talk things through. Where can I take you tonight after you finish up with Ty?"

The mention of the other man's name reminded her that Wes's friend would be returning any moment. She had an obligation to help Ty, and she wouldn't allow distracting thoughts of Wes to interfere with that. Still, she didn't pull away. Her scalp tingled on the other end of the hair he touched.

"Wherever it's busiest," she suggested, needing to see past the attraction to whatever motives had led Wes to tie her in knots again this week. "We can't let ourselves get sidetracked by the fireworks when there are real issues to consider first."

A smile hitched at Wes's mouth and his hand fell from her hair to trail down one arm. "Ever the practical one, aren't you?"

"Someone has to be." She appreciated the reminder of her role. She'd been playing it all her life with her mother. "I can't afford to drift along on insubstantial impulses that could disappear tomorrow."

Wes's brow furrowed as his fingers flexed lightly against her wrist. "Don't confuse me with someone else. There's nothing insubstantial about how I feel."

Emma wanted to remind him how fast he'd backed off their relationship in college, how easily he'd agreed that they would be better off pursuing their lives individually instead of as a pair. But behind Wes, footsteps sounded on the gravel pathway in front of the pole barn.

"Are we ready to roll?" Ty called out, his feet pounding double time. "I don't want to keep you long on a Friday." He skidded to a stop as he saw them together. "Oh. Hey, Wes. Want me to come back later?"

Wes eased back slowly, his hand falling away. His gaze lingered on her, though. "That won't be necessary. We were just firming up plans for later."

Emma nodded awkwardly, the loss of touch disconcerting when she'd been in tune to his every breath. "Right. Later."

"You think you'll be done in two hours?" Wes asked as he stood, his attention shifting to Ty who stood in the purple twilight with damp hair and a clean T-shirt paired with jeans.

"Definitely," Ty agreed with a nod. "I'm hoping to help Alexis with some spring planting in one of the greenhouses tonight. I've been trying to give her space this week, but with time running out before I leave for spring training, I figured she wouldn't say no to extra hands with the wildflowers."

Frowning at the thought of Alexis going to so much effort with the farm when she had her own physical therapy practice to run, Emma made a mental note to call her friend in the morning. Keely had asked Emma to keep an eye on Alexis—not that Alexis could know that—to make sure she didn't get too stressed in her caregiving role for their father. Alexis had a history with risk-taking when she got overwhelmed, and while planting in the greenhouse didn't sound risky, it also seemed like excess work she didn't need to undertake.

"I'll see you later then." Wes's voice intruded on Emma's worries, and his hand curved briefly around her shoulder in a light squeeze. "I'm taking you to The Hut," he said, referencing a third-generation barbecue place on Main Street. "We'll get some brisket and hash things out."

Emma struggled to ignore the flutter in her belly that made her want to tip her cheek against his hand. She needed to get herself together before this date. She wasn't interested in getting her heart broken again by this man with his restless feet.

"See you then," she murmured, feeling warmth crawl into her cheeks at the thought of being alone with him again.

For a split second, his thumb traced a path against the back of her shoulder, an evocative caress hidden from view. But then he was gone, stalking across the yard toward the main house.

Only then did she remember to breathe again.

Chapter Seven

AN HOUR LATER after showering and shaving, Wes stepped into the kitchen of the old country farmhouse. He'd been staying there since the holidays, though he'd been on his own for the last two weeks after his mother had jetted off to Andalusia for a cycling trip. Wes had offered to watch her dogs for her, but Cal's fiancée Josie had a soft spot for the two yellow Labs and Kungfu the Maltipoo after her job dog-sitting last spring, so Cal and Josie had taken the pups to their new place a little further south on Hickory Creek.

Wes's only responsibilities were to keep an eye on his mother's beehives, and to check on Everett in the house next door every day. More often than not, he ran into Cal doing the same thing, so Wes wasn't surprised to find his older brother at the kitchen counter now. Cal was prying open a box from a local restaurant, Char-Pie.

"You're dead, man," Cal muttered as he observed the contents. Or, more accurately, what was missing. "Coconut cream is Josie's favorite."

"Then you should have brought it home to her instead of leaving it here. I could only assume you wanted me to have it for breakfast." Wes reached into the fridge to retrieve the water pitcher before glancing out the back window to see how things were going at the study session in the backyard.

The sun had set, but the lights were on in the converted pole barn. Emma sat beside Ty in the glow of the overhead fixture, her auburn hair glinting with golden streaks. She pointed to something on a laptop screen, the silk sleeve of a blue kimono pooling in the table next to her. She wore it open over jeans and a lightweight leopard-print sweater, but Wes figured she had to be cold despite the patio heaters. The temperature had dropped since the sun had set.

"You're in training," Cal protested, opening the utensil drawer and pulling out a cake server. He jammed it under a slice of pie before relocating it to his plate. "The last I knew your routines were so hardcore, that meant you consumed nothing but superfoods and protein."

"Pie is a superfood. Ask anyone." Wes poured himself a glass of water and downed it.

In the past, he'd been vigilant about his diet and exercise all year, but especially in the weeks before the season started. He considered good health a tool to fuel athletic success, so it had never felt like a sacrifice to cut sweets, caffeine, alcohol, and a myriad of other things that many people indulged in regularly. But he'd definitely eased off some this year. He hadn't thought twice about having a beer when he took Emma to Hickory Hall, and he'd been the one to suggest s'mores the night of the bonfire at the Harper farm. Was he relaxing his approach because of Emma? Or was the reverse true, and he felt more relaxed around her?

"*I* know that," Cal protested, forking up a bite while still standing barefoot on the braid rug. "I just didn't think you did. In the future, I'll keep pies under lock and key." He barely took a breath before he continued, "So what's the deal with Emma? You two getting back together?"

Tension knotted across his shoulders. Were they? Emma had been keeping her distance this week, clearly wary about what might happen between them. And while he wanted to give her time to work out whatever she was feeling, he also wouldn't be in town much longer.

"If it's up to me, yes." Wes returned the water to the refrigerator and then moved toward the pegs near the back door to find a sweatshirt for Emma to wear. "I just have to convince her."

He rifled through team warm-up jackets from about six different baseball clubs—one dating back to someone's peewee season.

"She still doesn't like the idea of leaving Last Stand?" Cal asked, demonstrating a keener memory for Wes's personal life than Wes would have suspected.

Seizing a hoodie from his current team that he knew to be clean, Wes pulled it from the coatrack.

"Her mom hauled her all around the country before she came here. In sixth grade alone she was in three different schools." Wes hadn't forgotten her stories. The hardship of making new friends. The hurt of never saying goodbye because when Adeline made up her mind to do something, it had to be *that* minute or there were tears and drama.

"But she got her degree in San Antonio, right?" Cal persisted, dragging his fork across the plate so hard it squeaked. "So it's not like she can't live away from Last Stand."

Wes hadn't considered that before. But he also knew that his life on the road was chaotic at best. If Emma had resented pulling up stakes with her mom every few months until she arrived here, how would she handle being in a new city every few days?

"True." Although on the heels of that thought followed another. "Maybe her reluctance has more to do with not wanting to give up her life here to follow me around the country for my baseball career."

"Either way," Cal observed, pointing his fork in Wes's direction. "She has to like you first. Work on that part, and then worry about the rest."

"That's helpful, Cal. Thanks." Wes shoved through the back door to bring Emma a jacket, but not before Cal called after him.

"Everyone likes Emma, Wes," he called in warning. "Don't screw this up."

His brother's words echoed in his ears while the screen door slammed behind Wes. Mostly, Cal was giving him a hard time because, *brothers*. But he wasn't wrong. By embracing Last Stand, Emma had made a lot of friends here. She loved this town, and the town loved her right back. She was a committed English teacher and a frequent volunteer in the community. She'd joined the Daughters of Last Stand, and pitched in on whatever good works projects the group took on. In her free time, if she wasn't helping chaperone kids at Nate's baseball camp, she was watching her neighbors' dogs when they went out of town. Or—like now—teaching a frustrated friend how to conquer his illiteracy for good.

Ty and Emma were just pushing back from the table as Wes neared the pole barn. Something about their expressions made him stop in his tracks. Emma appeared troubled. Ty's rapid movements as he packed away his laptop and papers suggested he was upset. But over what?

"All done," Ty announced, slinging a duffel bag over his shoulder as he stood. "I'm officially a lost cause."

Emma rose, reaching toward him. "Ty, that's not true—"

But Wes read the guy's face easily before Ty strode quickly away.

"Let him go," Wes suggested quietly, stepping closer to Emma to wrap a reassuring arm around her shoulders. "He'll listen better once he cools off."

"I just suggested we try a different program that I thought would help him more." She was tense. Distressed.

He felt the stress vibrating through her muscles.

In the quiet yard, the sound of the door slamming on the garage apartment was like the crack of a gunshot.

Emma flinched, and Wes squeezed her closer. "You understand he's not mad at you, right?"

"I know." Some of the tension eased a fraction.

She dropped her head in defeat and he wanted to kiss the back of her hair. Or lay his cheek there. Maybe both.

Except comforting her was more important than what he wanted.

"He had high hopes he'd be able to really tackle this thing and get past it." Wes turned her in his arms so she faced him. "But there were bound to be setbacks. He knew that as well as anyone."

He'd spoken to Ty at length about the frustrations of not reading, and he'd gotten the impression Ty had never shared much about it with anyone else.

Emma sighed as she stepped away from him to gather up her tablet and notes, sliding them into a quilted pink sleeve of her bag.

"Maybe he did, but he liked the program we were using and felt comfortable that he understood how it worked." She carefully lined up the chair under the table, straightening the legs to match up with the seat beside it. "Then I introduced this whole new delivery system and he just retreated more and more until he finally said he was done trying to learn words that third graders knew."

She clutched her bag tightly, her knuckles white.

Wes hated that his friend had upset her, but he also empathized with the guy, who'd been through a lot. "He'll come around." He waited a long moment, but when she didn't speak, he couldn't help but ask, "Why the change in program if he liked the other one?"

"I wanted him to try one geared for dyslexia," she admitted, hitching her bag higher on her shoulder. "I think he'll make progress faster with different tools."

Reaching overhead to pull the chain on the ceiling fan fixture, Wes was distracted by a flash of lights across the pole barn.

Headlights.

"Someone just pulled in," Emma observed as she bent to turn off the patio heater, her auburn hair glinting fiery gold for a moment before she extinguished the flame. "Are you expecting anyone?"

For a moment he thought it could be Josie Vance, Cal's fiancée. But then the outline of an old van became clear, along with the Wildflower Farms logo on the side.

"It's Alexis." Wes hoped for Ty's sake the guy could pull himself together before he let his frustrations with himself wreck his hopes for a relationship with the smart, accomplished physical therapist.

"I wish he'd just tell her the truth about what he's doing," Emma confided in a soft voice as, together, they watched the shadow of the woman's figure emerge from the van and ascend the stairs to the second-story apartment.

"So do I." But Wes had enough trouble trying to convince Emma to take a chance on him. He wasn't arrogant enough to believe he had all the answers for Ty's relationship. "But he'll have to figure that out for himself. And in the meantime, you have a date with good barbecue."

He glanced down at her enough to see her high cheeks shift. He hoped she was smiling.

"I thought the date was with you?" she asked, her tone lightening a little. Giving him new hope for their evening together.

"I definitely plan to be there, too," he assured her. "I've been looking forward to spending time with you all day."

She peered up at him, meeting his gaze. "Then let's go."

Something shifted in his chest, the warmth of the attraction feeling a whole lot more than just physical. He took her hand as he led her across the damp grass toward his truck. And even though he wanted to simply focus on enjoying the feel of Emma's cool palm against his, he couldn't help but remember his brother's warning.

Don't screw this up.

He hoped like hell he wouldn't.

TAKING A DEEP breath, Alexis knocked on the door of the garage apartment behind the Ramsey family's house. She'd been expecting Ty at the greenhouse earlier, but he'd never shown up and hadn't called. That wasn't like him. Darkness had fallen over an hour ago, and the temperature had dropped enough to make her wrap a long, hooded sweater around her jeans and a logo tee for the flower farm. The front light was on—a black iron fixture that looked like it belonged in another century. She'd always loved the renovations the Ramseys had made to the Rough Hollow properties, no doubt spearheaded by Hailey Decker's discerning eye. One day, she hoped she could invest in the Harper place that way. She just wished her father could remain healthy enough to see those improvements happen. It was with bittersweet sadness that she acknowledged their relationship was better than ever now, when she didn't have long to spend time with him.

She knocked harder on Ty's door, needing to see him now that her dad was finally sleeping easily. This week had knocked her sideways, and she hadn't realized why it felt even tougher than usual until she'd realized that Ty had stopped coming around after the night of the barbecue with Wes and Emma. Then he'd blown off their plans together this evening.

The door opened then, spilling light out onto the small planked upper deck where she stood. Ty stood on the threshold looking even more tempting than she'd remembered from almost a week ago. His powerful shoulders were covered by a well-worn tee, paired with faded jeans. Seventies rock music flowed from the house along with the scent of lemon cleaner, as if he'd just tidied up the place. His hair fell heavier to one side of his forehead and he scrubbed it aside.

"Hey." His greeting was so spare that, in an instant, she recognized she hadn't been imagining his distance over the past week. "Sorry I didn't make it over tonight. I got busy."

After the ways he'd pursued her ever since the summer, making his interest clear, the step back took her by surprise. Although why should it when she'd been trying to keep things light between them?

Uneasiness mingled with regret at the very real consequences of keeping someone at arm's length. She bit her lip, understanding he might not invite her in.

"That's okay." She studied his blue-green eyes for a sign of his mood but couldn't read him. "Do you mind if I come in?"

"Sure." He seemed to shake himself, taking a step back into the apartment to admit her. "Sorry. I'm just surprised to see you here. I thought we were meeting at your place."

"It was getting late. I thought you'd forgotten." She followed him into a small living area next to a full kitchen, her tennis shoes padding silently along the slate tile floor. The place had a spare, masculine appeal, mostly white and gray with the occasional red accent.

"I got cleaning up and must have lost track of time." He moved toward a quartz countertop island separating the living room from the kitchen, and she would have done the same if her eye hadn't snagged on a black leather suitcase prominently placed near the front door. A silver laptop peeked out of a front pocket.

Alexis stopped in her tracks. "Going somewhere?"

Ty turned slowly, then nodded as he reached for a button on a counter-top speaker and switched it off. The music stopped. "Spring training starts next week. I figured I'd better get back to Houston to close up my apartment."

A jolt of panic spiked even though she had absolutely no right to feel it. Along with it came the adrenaline that had driven her to take ridiculous chances.

"So soon?" she ventured, hoping her voice didn't betray the swirl of emotions that had been flying more and more out of control ever since she'd moved back to Harper Farm. "I—I thought you were going to be here at least a few more days."

Ty's smile was wry. Unhappy?

"I may be a bit on the brash side, Alexis, but I'm not insensitive." His hand fisted on the quartz countertop, as if he didn't quite know what to do with it. "I hoped maybe if I stuck around long enough—showed you I could be committed to driving back and forth from Houston—you might give us a chance. But the off-season is coming to a close, and I'm no nearer to being someone you want in your life."

Shame filled her that she hadn't made time to talk to him about the pressure she felt taking care of her dad. Maintaining the flower business. She should have at least articulated that she needed more time to sort through her feelings.

"But we were supposed to get together tonight—"

"Only because I talked you into letting me help in the greenhouse. And I'm sorry I didn't call."

"I don't understand." She closed her eyes a moment to collect her thoughts. To check in with what she was feeling and make sure she was expressing herself the way she wanted. "That is, I realize I've been super cautious about getting involved, and I appreciate how respectful you've been of that." She licked her lips gone suddenly dry, hating that she might have hurt an incredibly nice guy in her own selfish need to keep herself safe. "But after how much time we've spent together, I'd hoped you would have at least let me know you were leaving."

He pounded his fist softly against the countertop. Once. Twice.

"Today was a frustrating day. I'm not sure what my plan was, actually."

Frowning, Alexis took a step closer, recognizing hurt when she saw it. She just wished she knew what was bothering him. It was a strike against her crap brand of friendship that she had no idea what he'd been up to in Last Stand for the past week.

"I'm sorry I haven't been a better friend." She didn't stop until she was a foot away from him at the island. "I should have checked in with you this week. But I hope it's not too late for us to find something fun to do together?"

His gaze flickered over her, the flare of male interest obvious. And, yes, welcome.

"I'm done with risk-taking behaviors, remember?" he reminded her. "You told me that was for the best when you were working out the kinks of all those broken bones and strained muscles from the motorcycle accident."

How well she remembered having her hands all over him. She swallowed, the air in the apartment turning sultry despite the cooling temperature outside.

"We don't need to skydive to have fun. I was thinking of a safer kind of thrill-seeking." Her heart hammered against her chest, hoping she was doing the right thing, but knowing she wasn't ready for him to leave.

Reaching the rest of the way for her hand, Ty brought it

to his lips and kissed her palm in a way that made her knees weak.

"As good as that sounds, you're not ready for that yet," he assured her, his voice stoking a fire inside her in spite of his words.

Or, hell. Maybe because of them. She couldn't deny the appeal of feeling safe with him. Like maybe this man understood her demons enough to help her battle them.

"But I'm not ready for you to leave," she told him, her words a feathery stroke of sound.

She liked Ty. Respected him and his easy understanding of who she was. She hated that she hadn't been there for him this week when he was shouldering problems of his own.

"You're sure about that?" He held her chin steady to look into her eyes.

"Positive."

"Then I won't." He folded her fingers around the place he'd kissed so she could hold it tight. "How about if we go for a drive? We can roll down the windows and air out the day, and then you can show me the best make-out places in town."

That startled a laugh from her, along with a rush of pleasure. And anticipation. With all the stress of the last weeks taking care of her father, growing her physical therapy business, and trying to keep her sister's wildflower business afloat, didn't she deserve a reprieve?

He still held her hand inside his.

"What makes you think I'd know any make-out places?"

she stalled. Or maybe she was flirting. It'd been so long since she'd tried it she almost forgot the dance of back and forth.

"You lived here during your teenaged years," he reminded her, pulling a set of keys off a hook near the back door. "I figured that qualifies you."

"I was an A student on track to graduate in record time." She'd pushed herself hard to make Keely proud. And yes, to get out of the toxic environment of their household. "There were no dating shenanigans on the weekend. Only study sessions."

"Then obviously, we've got a lot of lost time to make up for." He let go of her hand, but only to curl his strong arm around her waist and guide her toward the front door. "Shenanigans are my specialty."

Chapter Eight

"WHAT CAN I get for you?" Cole Hutchinson, one of the two barbecue brother proprietors of The Hut, asked Emma through a plume of smoke coming off the pit.

The scent of brisket and spices filled the air. She and Wes stood in the area designated for customers near the grill so patrons could see what was cooking. The restaurant had experienced a surge of popularity last year after a feature in *Modern Texas* magazine, and it was always crowded for the dinner hour. But after being delayed by the study session with Ty, Emma and Wes would have their choice of seating in the popular Main Street eatery.

And surely she could get through a shared meal without falling for him again. She wasn't in the market for a fling, and she knew that it would be impossible to have more than that with Wes when he was heading into spring training next weekend. Maybe a contrary part of her hoped that by dating him now that she was a little wiser, she wouldn't want him so much. So far, that seemed like a pipe dream. She was aware of him every second they were together.

"I'd like the pulled pork, please." Emma tucked her hands in the deep pockets of the hoodie Wes had given her at Rough Hollow.

The sweatshirt was from his freshman year of college, so she remembered it well. She'd worn it more than once while they'd been dating, and the memory of that time made her want to rub her cheek against the thick hood. The cotton smelled like fabric softener and cedarwood.

And when was she going to remember she wasn't a nineteen-year-old college student anymore? Dating had bigger risks now when the stakes were her home and heart. And—for her, at least—her future. She wanted to build a life with someone, not just indulge in short-term fun.

"I'm still craving the brisket, although everything looks good," Wes told Cole, before sliding a sideways glance toward Emma. "And you must want corn bread?"

"Of course," she assured him before smiling at Cole. "Thanks for the preview."

They moved away from the pit and headed toward the front counter. After placing the order, Wes led her toward a booth by the front window. Although it was dark outside, she could see the library lit up across the street, along with the statue of Asa Fuhrmann, the hero of Last Stand who'd helped defend the town in the Texas Revolution. Emma remembered seeing the statue her first day in town with her mom. They'd stopped for coffee and walked around the downtown to "get a feel" for the place so Adeline could decide if she wanted to stay.

"Did you know Last Stand was the first town that I chose, out of all the places my mom and I lived?" Emma asked as Wes took the seat across from her at the booth. A soft country ballad played from a speaker near the counter—atmospheric but not overwhelming.

"She let you pick?" Wes reached across the table to pick up her hand where it lay. He threaded his fingers between hers, then folded them together, locking their hands palm to palm.

"Well, she didn't ask me to choose. But she had a list of a few small Texas towns she thought could be fun, and Last Stand got my vote, thanks to Asa over there." She nodded toward the front window where the stern town hero kept guard over the main square in the municipal block of buildings. City hall, the courthouse, police station, and library took up the four corners around that statue.

Their food arrived then, and they spent a minute speaking to the woman who brought over their plates and drinks. Emma freed her fingers from Wes's, the feel of his touch lingering long afterward. She laid her napkin across her lap and dug in as soon as their server returned to the kitchen.

"So how did Asa win you over?" Wes asked while he drizzled honey on his corn bread.

"I liked the way his statue proclaims the town's history so proudly. We were in Last Stand for less than five minutes, and I already knew the story of how it got its name, and that Asa Fuhrmann risked his life to bring more ammo to the saloon from the trading post, in the process receiving the wound that would later take his life."

Wes grinned. "That's practically verbatim from the statue, isn't it?"

"Yes." She sipped her ginger ale with lime, the citrus a tasty counterpoint to the smoky-sweet flavor of the sauce on the pulled pork. "That little glimpse of history that day let me know that this was a town with roots it was proud of, and—what do you know—I'd been looking for a spot to put down roots I could be proud of too. So I started lobbying to make this our next home."

"And after that, you had to lobby every single year to stay," Wes observed quietly, remembering a fact she hadn't realized he would recall.

"By our third year here, she started taking off for a month at a time and just leaving me behind." She hadn't been scared for herself so much, but she'd worried that her mother might not return. "She got antsy staying in one place too long."

"Why do you think she's like that?" He shoved aside his phone when it beeped once, shutting off the ringer without ever even looking at the screen.

This man's undivided attention was a heady thing.

"You can take that—"

"No." Wes shook his head, his green eyes serious. "I'm here to be with you." He paused a moment, as if to let that idea sink in. Then he asked again, "Why do you think your mom has such a need to wander?"

Awareness hummed inside her as he shoved away everything else to focus on her. Wes was on the verge of a career break-through, something he'd waited for his whole life. But he asked about her as if her answer was the most important thing in his world.

"Mom will say it's because the world is too full of interesting people and places for her to spend her time in one spot." She clutched a hand to her chest as she said it, borrowing a little of the melodrama her mother liked to use when she made big declarations of life wisdom. "But I tend to think she changes the external because she can't change the internal. She *feels* different for a little while when she goes somewhere new, but inside, she's always the same Adeline."

"You've put a lot of thought into it." Wes studied her, a thoughtful expression in his green eyes.

How could he have thought otherwise? Her life had always felt transient while she'd been under her mother's control. But then again, maybe she'd tried so hard to fit in during her teen years that she hadn't voiced fears that her friends—even Wes—wouldn't identify with.

"Of course I did. It was a huge source of conflict for me my whole life, so I read as much as I could about people who move all the time." She took another bite of her dinner, telling herself not to dominate the dinner conversation.

Besides, they were venturing into the uneasy terrain of what happened when Wes left town again, and she wasn't ready to wade into that situation.

For a moment, they ate in silence. Then, Wes spoke again.

"Have you read about why other people resist moving?"

She exhaled to try and expel some of the tension knotting her shoulders.

"It's not that I *resist* moving," she reminded him, struggling to make herself understood. "It's more that I moved so many times I felt like a refugee before we came here, floating aimlessly with no sense of home." She'd been eager to make friends that would last more than a few months. To have a sense of routine and familiar things around her. "Plus, our moves were so far outside of my control. Mom made all the decisions about when and where to go."

"And you like being in control." Wes stabbed at his brisket, his simple silver wristwatch reflecting the pendant lamp over the booth.

"I like having agency over my own life. Who doesn't?" She finished her corn bread and shifted her plate aside, the heavy stoneware gliding over the polished table.

Wes remained quiet, and she could tell he was thinking. Or troubled. Maybe both.

"We all do," he said finally, then took a swig of his water. "But it's also a trade-off. I'd like to dictate where I live, but for as long as I'm in baseball, my team gets to decide for me. And I'm okay with that because I've made baseball a priority."

Her eyes wandered over him, thinking how different her life might be right now if Wes had decided to run Rough Hollow Farm instead of playing ball. For a moment, she imagined herself living in the Ramsey farmhouse with him. Being a part of his world and having him be a part of hers. Then, she blinked away the dreams that wouldn't happen and tried to keep her voice even as she replied.

"Which is fine for you because you're still choosing your priority. But what about for someone in your life who didn't make baseball a priority?" She folded her napkin into thirds and tucked it under her plate, wishing she could tidy up her romantic life as neatly. "Whoever is by your side has to make *you* the priority, while you're chasing a dream that's all yours."

He tipped his head to one side, as if studying her from a different angle would help. Had he honestly not thought of his life in that way? For as long as Wes chose baseball, the sport would dominate his partner's life. She'd been scared of that the first time they'd dated, and the fear hadn't gone away.

"It's only temporary," Wes protested. "A sports career doesn't last forever."

"So it's fine that someone else should delay their dreams in favor of yours?" Her heart rate sped up. She didn't like confrontation, and the conversation had gotten too pointed.

Uncomfortable.

"I honestly never thought about it in those terms." He gestured toward their empty plates. "Would you like anything else? Some dessert?"

"No, thank you." She appreciated the switch in topic since she hadn't meant to take on the issue of Wes's life once spring training began. He must see that any relationship continuing between them after this week would be impossible. "That was delicious, but I couldn't eat another bite."

They left the restaurant, and walked out onto Main Street. He convinced her to take a detour around the Asa Fuhrmann statue, to pay tribute to the town hero who'd been instrumental in convincing Emma that Last Stand was the right home for her. She'd thought he was content to let the subject drop about his life on the road, but as they walked back toward his truck, his arm slung enticingly around her shoulders, his jaw grazed her hair just above her ear before he spoke.

"I'd never expect you to delay your dreams for mine." The rasp of his voice hinted at the emotions underlying the words.

Or so she thought. Her skin tingled from the contact even as the declaration surprised her. Could he possibly mean that he would honor her journey as much as his own if their lives became intertwined again? She wasn't ready to pin him down on his words when she wasn't even sure what she hoped to hear.

Tucking the thought away, she couldn't help the anxious swirl of her emotions as she buckled into the passenger seat of his pickup.

Because all evening, underneath the thread of their conversation, had been the knowledge that they were on a date. A date that had started out with Wes's assurance that they'd keep a table and meal between them to ensure they talked before allowing things to get heated. Intimate.

Now, the meal was finished. The table was gone.

And she couldn't deny a jittery anticipation at the

thought of what might happen next.

She'd never been the kind of woman to indulge in a physical relationship for fun. Far from it. She'd needed a dating app to bring her into closer contact with men, and even then, she'd been more interested in a transactional arrangement than any fleeting, superficial pleasure. Yet Wes Ramsey wasn't just any man, and he stirred in her a whole range of complicated emotions along with a heady awareness she'd never felt around anyone else.

Those feelings—emotional *and* physical—were part of the reason she'd dodged seeing him again until this evening. But now, as they headed toward her home, her skin still on fire from when his jaw had brushed against her hair, she wasn't sure what she wanted. Another kiss that would scorch her insides and leave her wanting more?

Or—just this once—would she seek out the "more" with Wes and damn the consequences?

Once they reached Wes's pickup, he slid an arm around her elbow to slow her step. "I don't know about you, but I'm not ready to say good night just yet."

Immediately, her pulse triple-timed. Had he been thinking along the same passionate lines that she had been? Her skin warmed all over.

"It's still early," she agreed carefully, wondering what he had in mind.

She'd been looking for a sign to tell her where to go next with Wes, and she was determined to see this through until she found it.

"Would you mind going back to Rough Hollow for a little while?" His touch gentled, his thumb stroking the inside of her arm. Even through the layers of her lightweight sweater and the hoodie he'd loaned her, she could feel the warmth of him. "We could take a moonlight walk through the orchards. For old times' sake."

Nostalgia tugged at her at the mention of a shared activity from a lifetime ago. Nighttime strolls between the peach trees had been a way to be alone. And she couldn't deny that's what she craved now, too.

"For old times' sake," she repeated, unable to suppress a smile. "Let's go."

AN HOUR LATER, they'd walked the length of the peach orchard closest to the Ramsey farmhouse, sticking to the main trail between the upper east and west fields. At the end of the lane, a grove of loblolly pines made for tall, majestic shelter in the moonlight. A light breeze rustled the branches, the sound a subtle stirring in an otherwise quiet night.

Wes hoped the walk through the orchards would stir memories for her of how good they'd been together. It hurt to think of her turning him away again when what they'd shared had been so special. He wasn't ready to close the chapter on them yet. Beside him, Emma sniffed a sprig of mountain laurel flowers that he'd picked from a plant growing wild under the pines. The white flowers were one of the few things they'd seen in bloom on their walk, and Wes needed to text his mother to let her know about the plant since it was toxic for dogs. For that matter, if her bees found the flowers, the honey would be tainted too.

But right now, his focus was on Emma. The moon shown softly on her skin, casting everything in a pearlescent light. She'd been quiet since dinner, and he wondered what was on her mind. She tucked the flower stem into the teeth of the comb in her hair, a graceful touch.

"Don't you miss this during the season?" she asked as she turned to him suddenly, as if they'd been in the middle of a conversation. "The sights, the scents. It's so beautiful here, even in the winter when the trees are dormant."

"I miss it more than I used to." Wes took her hand in his to guide her back toward the farmhouse. The night was still cool, but the walk seemed to keep her warm enough. "For the first few years that I traveled with a professional team, I focused on how cool it was to be one step closer to my goal of playing in the majors. But after spending a couple of off-seasons playing winter ball and being on the road all year, I was eager to see Last Stand again."

"Have you and Cal made any progress convincing your grandfather to relinquish some control of Rough Hollow Farm?" She idly reached up to brush her free hand along a bare branch overhanging the gravel path between the orchards.

"No." He tamped down his frustration, feeling time slip away from him this week—both with Everett and with

Emma, too. "Everett is determined to wait for one of us—Nate, Cal, or me—to set aside baseball, and take over the farm operation for good."

"Do any of you have any interest in the business?" She ducked under a gnarled, low-hanging branch, her boots crunching in the gravel. "Do you?"

"Maybe." He hadn't shared the idea with anyone else since his baseball career was only just beginning. He hoped he could have many productive years ahead of him to contribute to a team. "Baseball players can have longer careers than some pro athletes, but even so, it's a young man's game. With luck, I hope to have ten good years ahead of me."

He could play longer than that, of course. But he was a realist. First he'd worry about securing his slot on a roster. Later, he'd concern himself with how long he could play.

"Everett will need help before then." Emma's fingers flexed gently around his hand, a wordless comfort to ease the sting of thinking about his grandfather's longevity.

Her kindness, thoughtfulness, was just one more reason he wanted to kiss her. Wrap her in his arms and show her how much he'd missed her.

Instead, he contented himself with giving her hand a return squeeze, then lifting hers to his lips to kiss the ridge of her knuckles.

"I know he will." He skimmed her smooth skin along his cheek. "Next I'm going to suggest a few changes to the land to scale back the production expectations and see if that helps take some pressure off him."

"Won't that cut profits?" She tipped her head skyward as a screech owl made its long, descending call, followed by a low trill.

He followed her gaze, the night sky clear through the tree branches.

"Not if I offer another way to make it up." He'd been tossing around ideas with Cal for weeks, but kept coming back to the one that seemed right for the Ramseys. "Seeing what Nate did in town with the baseball camp gave me an idea for turning some of the land into a farm camp for kids."

"Farm camp?" She turned surprised eyes his way as the lights from the house came into view. "I didn't know there was such a thing."

"Absolutely. Our catcher has kids and he sent his six-year-old son to one last year. The program emphasized seeing where their food comes from and learning about tending the land. I thought that would appeal to Gramp." Maybe even distract Everett from thinking he had to oversee the farming himself every day. "It could be good for the kids, and good for Gramp, too."

"That would be amazing, Wes. I already want to sign up to bring my ninth graders for a day. I'm a huge fan of activities outside the classroom for hands-on learning." She spoke enthusiastically about taking students into the field, from increased engagement to the interdisciplinary benefits and potential for bonding.

The idea clearly struck a chord for her, making him all

the more committed to the proposition. She slowed her step as they closed in on the backyard where exterior lights still gleamed on the garage apartment, as well as the main farmhouse.

He hesitated, still not ready for their night together to end. Hoping against hope that she wanted him as much as he wanted her.

Taking her hand in both of his, he nodded toward the side door. "Would you like to come in?"

She paused before she answered, and in that momentary space of time, Wes wished he'd thought to buy a pie so he could have offered her dessert. Given her some concrete reason to stick around.

But then she nodded, and something about her quick, decisive movement made him think she was feeling very definite about what she'd chosen.

"I'd like that." Her words were breathless, like she'd been running and only just now stopped.

The realization that she might be as nervous and excited as him tantalized him.

So he didn't let go of her hand as he drew her toward the quiet old farmhouse. Whatever else happened tonight, he was grateful for a little longer with the most enticing woman he'd ever met. With their time together ticking down to the day when he'd have to leave, he wasn't going to waste a second of it.

Chapter Nine

E MMA FOLLOWED WES through the back door of the farmhouse, telling herself that it wasn't truly a sign that they were meant to be together just because he'd dreamed up the most amazing, kid-friendly use for his family's farmland. Obviously, she liked the idea. Admired him for thinking of it. But it didn't have anything to do with her. Or mean anything for their future.

Still, she couldn't deny that it showed her another side of Wes. A thoughtful, warm-hearted side that he didn't show the world. No matter that he was relentlessly ambitious to achieve his baseball dream, there was much more to the man than his athletic career. It was enough to propel her into the Ramsey family's kitchen, a place she hadn't set foot in since the summer she'd broken things off with Wes. Immediately, memories flew at her from all directions.

How many times had she sat finishing homework at the scarred wooden table while waiting for Wes to return from practice? She used to love letting herself into the house like she belonged to their tight-knit family, plunking a backpack on a chair and chatting with Wes's mom while she baked cookies, fixed supper, or worked on her latest craft project.

Hailey Decker was so different from her own mother, an endlessly resourceful woman who embraced family and farm living.

Now, Emma peered around at the dark wood floors, bright braid rugs, and white cabinets, letting happy memories return.

"I remember I helped your mom build one of her first beehives right here." Striding deeper into the room, Emma ran her hand along the tabletop. "We used huge mason jars, and the bees built their honeycombs right inside them."

Wes shouldered off his sweatshirt, and hung it on one of the pegs near the back door. Then, he returned to her side while she unzipped hers. As she started to shrug out of it, Wes stepped behind her and helped her, easing the fabric down her arms. The silky kimono she'd worn over her own sweater clung to the sweatshirt as he peeled it away.

Sort of the way she wished she could cling to him. The thought sent shivers of awareness all through her.

"You can take the silk jacket too," she murmured, tempted to arch back against his touch where his fingers moved to separate the fabrics. "It was purely decorative."

"It's pretty." Wes sounded sincere, although she could hear the smile in his voice as he turned to hang up both garments on the wooden pegs. "Just like everything you wear. I almost never see you in a T-shirt and jeans."

She couldn't help a wry laugh. "That's my mother's influence. Mom says life isn't a dress rehearsal, so there's no sense wearing anything that isn't ready to take center stage."

Emma's gaze wandered over Wes's big, solid frame as he rejoined her, her breath catching at the sight of his muscles hugged by the gray cotton Henley he wore.

"I never told you this, but I used to like looking for you at school every day to see what you'd be wearing." He stopped a few inches from her, standing almost toe-to-toe so that she forgot to breathe. "I'd make bets with myself if it would be turquoise or purple, but then you'd come in wearing a belted white T-shirt for a dress, but with pink sunglasses that had palm trees on them."

He stared down at her with those deep green eyes of his, as if he liked what he saw. Liked what he remembered. She hadn't known he'd paid attention to details like that. The idea made her wonder what else she'd overlooked about him. She'd known he was a quiet, intense, driven man. But she hadn't known that quiet intensity had been so thoroughly directed toward her when they'd dated.

"I remember those sunglasses," she admitted, her breath catching to have him so close to her. To realize that she'd taken up more space in his memories than she'd ever suspected. "My mom loved to shop at flea markets. It was one of the few extravagances we could afford." She paused, shaking her head. "Never mind. I'm babbling."

He stroked her with his eyes, if not his hands. Yet. "Keep talking. I want to hear."

She gauged his expression for signs he might be placating her or teasing her. But his gaze was filled with sincerity.

"Okay, then." She swallowed past a wad of nerves.

"Mom would flirt her way through the tables, haggling for better prices, and sometimes she'd come home with whole boxes of oddball things. So, in the beginning, I was wearing retro dresses with a camera bag for a purse because I had to. It used to bug me that I couldn't just go to the Gap like everyone else, but Mom would say, 'Baby, who wants to be average?'"

Funny to think about that now after the frustrating conversation with her mother the week before when Adeline had tried to convince her to visit the West Coast for spring break. Reminiscing about her mother's ability to spin something from nothing made her realize how infrequently she let herself think about the good times she'd shared with her mom. Wes had given her that gift.

"You were never average." His unconditional affirmation touched her.

Then, suddenly, his fingers did too. He brushed them experimentally over her cheek, igniting a whole chain reaction of sensations. Heat flushed her face and neck. Her belly flipped, pulse fluttering. Not just from the touch, but from the warmth in his green eyes, a light that only came into his expression when he looked at her.

She struggled for the words to reply, but rational thought had flown the moment the callused pads of his fingers grazed her skin. Or maybe the moment she'd realized that his memories of her were rooted in a deep recognition of who she was as a person. Had anyone ever known her as well as Wes Ramsey? Certainly, she'd never let anyone else into her heart.

Now, she could only breathe in the cedarwood scent of him as he hovered nearer, his broad shoulders blocking everything else from her vision. Her hands landed on his upper arms without her conscious thought. Beneath the thin cotton of his Henley, his muscles shifted.

She couldn't have said who initiated the kiss. But one moment she stood hypnotized by sensual memories, and the next, their lips met. Pleasure stirred at the feel of his mouth on hers, and she savored the gentle glide of his tongue coaxing entrance. She sucked in a sigh and his arms banded around her, drawing her fully against him.

The contact electrified her. The feel of his solid strength made her weak with want, her body attuned to every subtle shift of his. Her fingers flexed, nails dipping into his flesh through the soft barrier of cotton his shirt provided.

He kissed her again and again. And again. He took his time showing her how much he enjoyed just that one act, until she was humming with the need for more. Far more. When his lips drifted to the side of her mouth, and down her neck, she thought she'd come out of her skin for want of more. More of the feel and taste of him. If she hadn't shifted her feet and grazed her thigh against the table, she might have even forgotten where they stood.

In the middle of the kitchen farmhouse, devouring one another.

"Wes, wait." She broke away from him with an effort, her breasts aching as he ran his hands over her hips, up and down.

He could turn her inside out with just that simple touch.

"I could kiss you all night," he vowed, his green eyes a shade deeper in the half light from a dimmed pendant lamp over the counter. "Or I could do anything you want." The hands on her hips stopped, his fingers pressing ever so slightly against her curves. "Tell me, Emma. What do you want?"

Her pulse began to rush all over again, the throb in her ears a mirror of the pulsing of anticipation in her belly.

She knew decisions like this were best made without the suggestive persuasion of awareness flooding her veins. But she hadn't gone into the evening with a plan for intimacy. She'd only hoped to find a sign that they were meant to be together. Or not. And she couldn't possibly justify this supercharged sensation as a sign, could she?

"I want you to remind me how good we could be together." The words tripped from her lips without her permission, an honest thought even if she hadn't meant to share it.

Wes circled her waist with his hands. "Nothing could give me more pleasure."

Then, with seemingly no effort, he lifted her against him and carried her into a darkened bedroom at the back of the house. The air was cooler here, the room slightly scented with lavender. She had a vague impression of gray furnishings and white walls, woven accents and a natural fiber rug covering the dark hardwood. Wes closed the door behind them with his foot, so that the only light came in through a high transom window left uncovered above French doors to the exterior porch.

He lowered her slowly to her feet, taking his time so that she felt every nuance of his body skimming along hers. Her curves molding to his heat and strength as he stared into her eyes, seeing pieces of her she'd never shared with anyone else.

"I've missed you," he told her when her toes hit the ground. Then, when he released her completely, she felt the edge of the bed against the back of calves. "More than you know."

Jittery anticipation made her breathing shallow. She hadn't allowed herself to contemplate what it might be like to be in his arms again. Now, faced with the prospect, she understood why. She hadn't truly given herself to anyone else but him. She'd tried—there'd been two intimate relationships since him and they'd both been underwhelming. But she'd never really let her guard down, let alone experienced the same kind of sensual connection as she'd once shared with this man.

She didn't want to place too much emphasis on the undeniable chemistry. And yet, by ignoring the role it played in a relationship, was she doing a disservice to the guys she'd planned to date for expediency's sake? A disservice to herself, for that matter? The thought crumbled one of the foundations she'd been building her pragmatic future on.

"I've missed this. Missed you," she admitted, her voice uneven with too many emotions that she wanted to shove aside to focus on the moment.

"Emma." He traced the lines of her face, seeming to read every nuance of her expression with his fingertips. They trailed over her jawline. Her lips. "You're shaking. Are you sure this is what you want?"

She nipped his thumb between her teeth and held it long enough to make her point. Or maybe long enough to let go of all the damnable practicality that usually guided her. She swirled her tongue around his thumb for good measure, tracking his green gaze as desire leapt in his eyes. When she spoke again, she let her certainty come through.

"Very sure." She arched into him, threading her arms around his neck and pulling him down to her for another kiss.

His mouth melted into hers, setting her body on fire with every stroke of his tongue. Every shift of his lips gliding over hers. She tilted her head, deepening the kiss. Needing to give him full access to her. She'd forgotten how sexy a mating of mouths could be. The kiss brought her body flush against his, and the contact tantalized her, making her hungry to feel still more of him.

When at long last he came up for air, he slid his hand beneath the hem of her sweater to cup her waist. "I'd like to undress you."

A shiver tripped up her spine at the prospect.

"Not as much as I'd like to undress you." Her fingers walked up his chest and her whole hand smoothed the way back down, reveling in the feel of the impressive expanse of muscle.

A shudder rippled through him, and she marveled that she could do that to him—give him back a fraction of what she was feeling.

"I seriously doubt that." He flicked open the button at the waist of her jeans before parting the zipper. He palmed the curve of her belly, his pinky finger grazing lightly over the satin of her panties.

She blinked through the haze of yearning, too wound up to argue over something she wanted anyhow. Instead, she gripped his shoulders tighter and gave herself up to the moment. To him.

With a wriggle of her hips, she helped him lower the denim until it was off. He skimmed her sweater up and over her head too, leaving her in a lace camisole. Then he tipped her back onto the bed, joining her there.

All that time, her breathing hitched faster. She stared up at him as he positioned himself over her, letting her feel the weight of his body. Then he shifted to one side, making himself comfortable next to her while his hand drifted all around her mostly nakedness. Relearning her curves. Exploring what made her breath catch.

His touch was unhurried. Focused. He'd forgotten nothing about what she liked, and he used it to his advantage now. No, to her advantage. Because this is what she'd asked for—a reminder of what it was like between them. And…wow.

He delivered.

His lips closed over her breast through the lace camisole,

while his hand dipped between her thighs. Her every nerve ending was hyper aware of him, his touch precisely in tune with her body. His fingers circled, mimicking the flick of his tongue around her nipple. She couldn't help the whimper of need that touch elicited. Her fingers twisted in the fabric of the duvet, her legs twitching restlessly. Hungrily. When he edged back to rake his hot green gaze over her body, she couldn't stifle the urge to grip his wrist and hold him right where she wanted him. Only then did he touch her the way she most needed, his hand finally sliding beneath the satin of her panties. His thigh trapped hers, holding her still for the sensual onslaught. Her breath caught. The tension in her gathered tighter and tighter until he sent her catapulting over the edge.

Waves of pleasure dragged her under, holding her down. And they weren't even naked yet.

❧

WES HAD NEVER seen anything more beautiful than Emma when she forgot everything else but herself. She selflessly gave her time and talents to so many others through her job and the good works that came so naturally to her. So it was a privilege to see her this way, with her guard down, taking something just for her.

With her cheeks flushed, hair tousled, and lips slightly swollen from his kisses, she was temptation incarnate.

"Wow." Her voice whispered along his cheek as she

turned to him where he lay beside her.

"My thought exactly." He held himself back, even though the need to be with her was an insistent hunger. He wouldn't let his own desire distract him from what he wanted most—making Emma see what they could have together.

He contented himself with kissing her through the lace of her camisole, lingering on the dark shadows of her nipples until her back arched. Her fingers trailed restlessly over his shoulders, every now and then clenching tight and holding him close.

She pried her blue eyes open to study him in the pale moonlight spilling over the bed from the high transom window.

"How come only one of us is mostly naked?" Her exploring fingers tunneled beneath the hem of his shirt to splay over his bare chest. "I think if *I* was the professional athlete, I would be glad for any excuse to show off my hard work in the gym."

She trailed her fingers lower to trace along his obliques.

And damned if her touch didn't act like gasoline on the fire already simmering inside him.

"Emma." He captured her wrist and held her fast, willing the heat to die down. "It's been a long time for me."

His focus had always been on his game, not the added attention from women that some of his teammates indulged in.

She stilled beneath his touch until he let her go. Then

she spoke softly into his ear. "I'm not going anywhere tonight. So we can get the first time out of the way and then do it all over again. More slowly."

It was tough enough fighting his own instincts. He couldn't deny her what she wanted.

"I'm holding you to that." Easing away from her, he stood long enough to divest himself of his clothes and find a condom in the bathroom connected to the guest bedroom.

When he returned Emma was in the middle of peeling off the camisole, leaving him dry-mouthed and even more ready to have her. He wasted no time sheathing himself before he joined her on the bed. Locking eyes with her, he made room for himself between her thighs. With every breath he drew, he remembered how fortunate he was to be with this woman. To be entrusted with her body. Her pleasure.

When at last he eased inside her, he knew there was no place he'd rather be. No other woman for him. He'd known it even before tonight. But now, the past and the present merged, all his best memories bound up with this woman along with his hopes for the future.

He tilted her hips up, needing to lose himself in her. Again and again they moved together, in perfect synch. She'd been the first woman he'd ever been with. Now, he wanted her to be the last.

He just needed to show her that he meant it.

Rolling onto his back, he took her with him, seating her on top. Moonlight outlined her, giving her an ethereal glow as she tossed her head back and found a rhythm that suited her. She moved faster. Slower.

She bit her lip and rolled her hips as she stared down at him, testing her own power. Pushing him to the brink too fast. But damn, did he love the way she did that. He felt his release close at hand, and he reached between them to touch her again, to tease her body into the frenzy she'd felt earlier.

A soft cry escaped her, and she held perfectly still for a long moment. Then her legs collapsed beneath her. Her hips slid even closer to his, sealing them together.

And that did it. More than what he felt, just seeing Emma find pleasure was a bigger turn-on than anything else he'd ever known.

Completion roared through him. Every square inch of him felt the pull of her body as she contracted around him. Squeezing. Pulsing.

The moment spun out, his mind blanking for long moments while sensations rolled through him.

After a while, he gathered her to him, and they lay side by side on the guest bed. Eventually, their speeding pulses returned to normal. He wasn't sure his heart did, however. He could feel it making a place for this woman. Or maybe the place she'd occupied had always been there, just waiting for her return.

But even as he stroked Emma's hair and looked forward to being with her again, he suspected that she was as busy making plans to hold him at arm's length even as he was plotting to reel her in.

This time, for good.

Chapter Ten

E MMA WOKE TO the sound of a dog barking.

Blinking the sleep from her eyes, she had a moment's panic that she'd forgotten about a dog-sitting job. Was she supposed to be watching Sasha today, her neighbor's Siberian retriever mix?

But then the farmhouse room came into view around her, with the gray bed linens, white walls and dark floors. The pillow next to her was vacant in the queen-sized bed, but Wes had been beside her as recently as a couple of hours ago. She remembered him kissing her neck before he went on a pre-dawn run. Now, the sun was high enough that it had to be midmorning—a testament to how little she'd actually *slept* during her night with Wes since she was usually up much earlier than this. Her whole body felt sated. Although her brain already wanted the answers to pesky questions like what was she doing sleeping with a man who was set to leave at week's end?

A man she'd already hurt once by breaking things off between them?

Deep woofs mingled with high-pitched yaps outside the bedroom window. Curious, she leaned toward the sill to peer out when she heard male voices. Wes and—was that his brother Cal?

Scrambling out of bed, Emma pulled a travel toothbrush from its case in her purse. The habit was left over from a lifetime ago when her mother had made her leave one home after another—oftentimes with nothing more than the clothes on her back—as they dodged irate landlords. As Emma brushed her teeth and ran a comb through her hair, she promised herself she'd call her mom today. She hated that their last conversation had been an argument about Emma's spring break plans.

She owed Keely a call too. But she wasn't sure how much she could say to her friend about Alexis working day and night without feeling like she'd betrayed a confidence.

Padding back into the bedroom, she peeked into a bureau drawer and found a stack of clean T-shirts. She grabbed a bright blue one, recognizing the logo for one of Wes's former Double-A teams—a semi-fierce-looking shrimp from his days in Jacksonville. Pairing it with yesterday's jeans, she strode into the kitchen to slip on her boots and grab a sweater from the long row of wooden pegs near the back door.

Before she could step outside, however, a bark sounded from the front of the house. Emma spun on her heel to go that way, opening the front door at the same time she caught sight of a dark-haired beauty sitting cross-legged on the porch swing with a book in her hands. A fluffy white dog leapt to its feet on the green cushion beside the woman, while two yellow Labs flanking the swing at her feet only thumped their tails in greeting.

"Morning," the woman greeted her as she laid down a tattered copy of a Toni Morrison novel, and placed a soothing hand on the barking dog's back. She shushed it with a word, then extended her free hand toward Emma. "I'm Josie Vance, Cal's fiancée. And you probably already know Hailey's dog, Kungfu."

Petite and curvy, the woman had a ready smile and pretty, delicate features. She wore her dark hair twisted in a haphazard way, so the ends stuck out at angles from a tortoiseshell clip. Her pink yoga pants and long black sweater were casual, but her left hand bore a glittering pear-shaped diamond in a platinum setting.

"Emma Garcia." Emma held out her hand, and they shook despite the subtle rocking of the swing. She didn't know how to label herself—Wes's ex-girlfriend? overnight guest?—so she didn't try. "Nice to meet you. Where are the guys?"

The other woman pointed to the house next door while the little dog beside her settled back down, resting its muzzle on her thigh. "They joined forces to talk Everett into Wes's farm camp idea. Cal was supposed to meet me for breakfast after he went running with Wes, but then when he heard Wes's idea for the camp, he wanted to approach Everett with it while they were together. They just left a minute ago."

"Do you think Everett will go for it?" Emma asked, leaning down to scratch the yellow Lab closest to her. Keely had told Emma that Josie had been the caretaker for the Ramsey house last spring, and had befriended the older man then.

"Hard to say," Josie mused, folding her legs under her. "Mostly, Everett just wants one of his grandsons back home full-time to take charge of Rough Hollow. But maybe if he sees that Wes and Cal are behind the plan—or if he thinks they'll come back to Last Stand more often because of the camp—then he might approve the idea."

Emma walked deeper onto the porch so she could see the house next door better. Everett's home was older, a stone structure with deep overhangs to keep the place cool in the summers before air-conditioning. There was no movement over there now, not even a vehicle in the driveway, although she saw a fancy sports car parked in front of the farmhouse, which she assumed must be Cal's since it had California plates. Wes's older brother had been picked up by the Oakland team last season.

"Congratulations on your engagement, by the way." Emma tugged at the hem of her T-shirt, wishing she'd been a little better prepared for meeting a stranger in Wes's house this morning. "I'm good friends with Keely Harper, Nate's girlfriend, and she told me about how you and Cal met."

Josie tipped her head back and laughed. "Did she tell you I held him at gunpoint when he walked right into his mom's house, not knowing I was there the first night? Definitely an awkward start, but it all worked out in the end."

She wanted to ask *how* things worked out, how two people could negotiate a future when it meant one of them had to give up their dream for the other? But she knew the obstacles in Cal's and Josie's path weren't necessarily the same ones that blocked Emma's way forward with Wes.

So instead, leaning against the porch rail, she settled for asking, "You don't mind life on the road?"

"I like life with Cal wherever he is." The warmth in Josie's voice as she spoke of her fiancé was impossible to miss. "And it's not really life on the road so much as rotating between three homes—a condo in Florida for spring training, Cal's house in Oakland for the regular season, and then last fall we bought a spot in Last Stand for the off-season."

Emma tried to imagine herself only returning to Last Stand for part of the year. And while maybe it would still feel like home after so many months away, what about her teaching? She loved her job, and she was good at it. Even if she moved to a new city to meet eligible bachelors—the way she'd contemplated if her dating scheme didn't work out—at least she'd be living in the same place year-round and could be in the classroom.

"What do you do when Cal has away games?" Emma knew that half of a player's 162 games each year were on the road. That meant two and a half months of life in hotels during the regular season.

"So far, I haven't traveled with the team, but Cal was only on the Oakland roster for half of last season." Josie paused to adjust her hair clip, twisting the long rope of dark hair before closing the tortoiseshell clamp around it again. "I used that time to return to Last Stand, check on Everett and house-hunt. But this year, I'm definitely going to explore more cities when Cal has road games."

"That's what Keely did last year." Emma hadn't spoken to her friend very often since she'd decided to leave Last Stand and travel with Nate Ramsey. But Keely had posted photos from Boston and New York, Miami and Los Angeles in her social media. She looked happy in all of them, but then, Keely had only stayed in Last Stand to take care of her alcoholic father struggling with advanced liver disease.

It was easy to see why Keely's heart would be lighter once she left home. Whereas Emma had already seen all those cities. She already knew happiness was here, in Last Stand.

"Are things getting serious between you and Wes?" Josie asked, leaning forward a little on the swing seat. "Are you considering giving it a try? We could meet up when Cal and Wes play each other. For that matter, Oakland and San Francisco are so close we'd see each other even at home—"

"No." Emma shook her head, needing to cut off the idea before Josie shared it with Cal or it got back to Wes somehow. "It hurt the last time we broke things off because we didn't know how to reconcile our lives." She bit her lip, recognizing that had been her doing and not his. She'd shut down their relationship, afraid of being left behind once he had his chance at the big leagues. "I'm really not sure where this is heading."

Which meant she probably shouldn't have spent the night with Wes. But dating didn't come with rule books. And she found it tough to regret being in his arms, no matter if things ended between them when he got on the flight for Arizona.

"I understand." Josie's voice was kind, her blue eyes sympathetic. "Better than you think. I stumbled more than once figuring out how to be with Cal, and it hurt."

Emma was about to ask her more, but her cell phone chimed with "Build Me Up Buttercup," the ringtone she'd assigned Keely, her wildflower-farming friend. Emma would have simply turned off the ringer, except it struck her as unusual that Keely would call this early on a Saturday morning.

"Will you excuse me for just a minute?" she asked Josie. At the other woman's nod, Emma hit the button to connect the call.

"Emma? Oh thank goodness you answered," Keely blurted the words in a rush, her voice thready. Emotional. "Alexis just messaged me that Dad fell down the stairs this morning and she couldn't rouse him afterward. She said she was taking him to the emergency room, and I'm just so worried—"

"I'll go to the hospital right now," Emma assured her. She didn't have a car, but she could call for a ride straight there.

"Would you? Alexis isn't answering her phone, but she could still be in the ambulance or maybe she's driving him herself?" Keely spoke quickly, sounding distressed. "Or she might have had to power down if she's in a room with him."

"I'll call you the second I know anything," Emma promised, knowing how hard it had to be for her friend to be away from her family in a crisis. Keely's only fear about leaving Last Stand had been if something happened to her father. His prognosis was poor. "I can be there in half an hour, tops."

From the Ramsey farmhouse, the hospital was a quick drive, even if she had to wait for a ride.

"Thank you, Emma. So much."

Disconnecting, Emma was already heading toward the front door. "I'm sorry, Josie, but I need to get to the hospital. That was Keely and her father—"

But Josie was already on her feet and bringing the dogs into the house. "I'll drive you. Let's go."

INSIDE HER FATHER'S private room at Gordon C. Jameson Hospital, Alexis tried to pace off the anxiety churning through her, the sick feeling increased by the antiseptic smell and the recycled air. The latest physician had just left them, her attempts to reassure Alexis falling flat since it had boiled down to this—Dad was too advanced in his liver disease to risk surgeries.

Her gaze cut to the bed where her father now slept, his form greatly shrunken since her childhood where he'd shouldered the burden of raising two girls alone after his wife had left the family. For a few years after they moved to Last Stand, he'd been the best champion she could imagine for newly motherless girls. Then, he'd started drinking.

By the time Alexis had gone to college, her dad had already been wiry and thin. Now, in the last six months that she'd been living with him full-time, he'd lost at least ten more pounds on a frame that couldn't stand to lose an ounce. It made him frail and vulnerable when he'd fallen down the staircase this morning. The noise had been terrifying.

Lowering herself to her father's bed, the bleached blankets stiff beneath her, she laid a hand on his arm just above his identification bracelet. He was already covered with bruises. One arm was splinted, and he wore a neck brace strictly as a "precaution" since the X-ray hadn't shown a break there.

She was too rattled to call Keely with the latest update. Emma and Josie had arrived an hour ago, after she'd already texted her sister the preliminary news—he had a broken arm and fractured hip, but the biggest fear was internal bleeding that they continued to monitor. Emma and Josie had left Jimmy Harper's room when the latest doctor had arrived, but they'd promised to return after a quick trip to the cafeteria.

Alexis assumed it was them when the wide door to the room opened a moment later.

"Alexis?" Ty stood there instead, framed in the open door while a nurse hurried down the hallway, balling up a sterile gown as she went. "Is it okay to come in?"

The mix of emotions that went through her at the sight

of him was too confusing to wade through, knotting in her chest along with all the fears she had for her dad. But the sharpest sensation was relief. She was glad to have his strength beside her while machines beeped, and doctors were paged out in the busy hospital corridor.

"Yes. Please." She nodded, blinking fast to try and rein in her runaway feelings. "Thanks for coming."

"Emma texted me that you were here with your dad," he explained as he let the door shut behind him, quieting the room of everything but her father's soft snores. Walking over to the bedside, Ty took the seat across from her in a big armchair near the rolling table with her handbag and some paperwork. "How is he?"

Ty reached for her free hand and held it between his own, the touch reminding her of the fun time they'd had together the night before. They'd ended up going out for ice cream and driving along the river. They hadn't ended at a make-out point, but Ty had stopped in a park and kissed her anyhow.

Their relationship that had started with so much sizzle—her hands learning every inch of his athletic body in her physical therapy work—had shifted to something deeper. Something that scared her in its intensity, even as it beckoned her closer. The draw of this man went far beyond sexual chemistry, even if his kisses turned her inside out. With an effort, she stuffed away those memories to focus on his question.

"He's stable, according to the doctors." She'd wanted

this time in Last Stand to spend more days with her father, knowing he didn't have long to live. Even so, she hadn't really prepared for the end. "But it doesn't take a medical professional to see—"

She gestured vaguely toward her dad's gray pallor, her sentence ending in a distressed sound she couldn't swallow back.

"I'm sorry." Standing, Ty wrapped her in his arms and pulled her against his broad chest, exactly where she wanted to be. He stroked her back through her hair, his lips pressed to her forehead while he held her.

For a long while she simply breathed in the sandalwood scent of his aftershave, taking all the comfort she could from his nearness. His warmth.

"I just wanted more time with him," she murmured into his chest where she'd made his shirt damp with tears she hadn't meant to shed. "These last months have gone so fast between starting the new practice and getting Keely's wildflower farm back in order."

There'd been a fire at Windy Meadows last summer, set by Jimmy Harper trying to resurrect an old still. Luckily, he'd been unsuccessful, and his sobriety remained intact. Not so luckily, he'd destroyed some of Keely's fields and a storage barn with a refrigerated room where she stored cut blooms.

"But you're here with him now," he reminded her, holding her at arm's length to look into her eyes. "You rearranged your whole life to come back home. Any father would be glad to have a daughter like that."

Her chest ached at Ty's kindness. His thoughtfulness. Except he was becoming so important to her, and that scared her at a time when she was already hip-deep in her fear of losing her dad.

She'd been to enough Al-Anon meetings to understand that it wasn't just about her father. She'd thought she'd healed from the old hurt of her mom's abandonment, but the deep fracture inside her throbbed now. And it had Ty's name written all over it. Because why would a successful baseball player at the height of his career ever stick around Last Stand, Texas, to be with a woman who wanted to spend every moment possible with the dad she was sure to lose this year?

"Maybe." She edged back from him, trying to get ahold of herself. "But it's hard to say what is important to my father anymore. He's retreated into himself a lot since the fire."

She knew part of it was simply that his health was deteriorating. Still, it hurt not to know that she might not have any more meaningful conversations with him. That she might never understand him better. Feeling vulnerable, she paced the room, needing to excise the overload of worries.

For a moment, Ty said nothing. Still, his gaze followed her. Thoughtful. Assessing.

"What if you had more help on the farm so you could spend that time with your dad?" Ty asked, shifting back into the armchair near the bed.

"Not in the budget." She shook her head.

"Let me help you." He stood, coming toward her with a determined glint in his blue-green eyes. "I can at least get the barn repaired before I leave."

The reminder of his imminent departure only twisted the aching knot in her. The pain of being without him was going to hurt so much more than she'd thought. He'd come to mean more to her than she'd realized, even though she'd tried her best to steel herself against those feelings.

"I can't think about the barn right now," she burst out, knowing her focus had to be on her father. "I tried to tell you last night that I want to explore this thing between us too, but I don't have the emotional resources to navigate whatever this is between us right now. I can't. I just...can't."

She broke away from him, knowing she wasn't being fair, but her coping skills for stress were limited. She'd always dealt with her father's alcoholism by working harder or by taking risks. The latter was off the table, and the former was grinding her into the ground. She understood what she was doing wrong, she just wasn't sure how to stop herself from repeating old patterns that didn't work anymore. And how could she invite Ty into her life when she didn't have herself figured out yet? She stared out the hospital room window, unseeing.

When Ty spoke again, there was a gravity she'd never heard from him. "I'm not asking for anything more than to be with you. I care about you. Deeply."

The revelation pushed hard at her defenses, all but breaking them. She didn't dare meet his eyes or she'd be lost. And she needed to hold herself together now. For her father's sake.

For her own.

Dragging in a deep breath, she steeled herself against the insistent tugging at her heart.

"I care about you, too." She didn't want to hurt him. But how much could she give him? Maybe she'd been selfish to ask him to stay the night before. "It's just that I have a really painful time in front of me, Ty. Do you see those papers next to the bedside?"

He was silent for a moment, and she had to look up to check that he was still close to the armchair where the printed file for a Do Not Resuscitate order awaited her review. Her signature.

Ty remained there, his gaze on the very papers she meant. His expression blank.

Uncomprehending?

"You see what I mean?" she asked, wondering if he didn't make the connection between what Ty was asking and what she faced with her father's health. "I just don't know how much I can give right now. Not with what's ahead for Dad."

But the lines of Ty's face didn't soften. If anything, his lips flattened. His jaw tense. A flare of something al-most…angry?…flashed in his eyes. Surely she was misreading him.

Except that he pivoted on his heel and walked out of the hospital room.

Stunned, Alexis watched him go, wondering what the

hell had just happened. Had she offended him by not taking his offer of help? She'd tried to make it clear she reciprocated his feelings, that she just wasn't sure how to be in a relationship right now.

She didn't have one single clue what she'd said that had been so wrong, but whatever had happened felt like it clawed the tattered bits of her heart out. So it was a damned good thing she hadn't let herself fall in love with him.

Oh wait... something soft inside her whispered as a wave of pain took hold of her and squeezed.

Too late.

Chapter Eleven

WES HAD JUST parked his truck and was jogging toward the main entrance of the hospital when he spotted Ty charging from the place like he was running from a tag-out.

"Slow down, man," Wes greeted him, stepping into Ty's line of sight. "Any news on Alexis's dad?"

Wes had seen the message from Emma about Jimmy Harper after his conversation with his grandfather about the possibility of allocating some of the Rough Hollow lands to a farm camp. Everett hadn't embraced the idea, but he hadn't completely dismissed it either, which was about as good of a reaction as Wes could have hoped for. Cal was on his way to the hospital too, since Josie had texted him as well, but Wes hadn't seen his car pull up yet. Now, Wes dodged an orderly pushing an older man in a wheelchair, and then ducked under a rogue balloon bouquet carried by a little girl too busy talking excitedly to her parents to watch where she was going.

Ty seemed oblivious to all of it, including Wes, as he kept plowing forward.

"Ty. Seriously." Wes put a hand on his friend's shoulder

as he noticed the dark look on Ty's face. "What gives? Is Jimmy Harper okay?"

With clear reluctance, Ty halted on the sidewalk, shaking his head. "I have no idea."

"What do you mean? Isn't he in there? Did you see Alexis?" Wes peppered him with questions, unable to account for Ty's expression, let alone why the guy would be leaving Alexis's side now when he'd done everything in his power to get closer to her over the last months.

Heaving a frustrated sigh, Ty palmed the top of a parking meter, his grip so hard it made him white-knuckled.

"I saw her," he acknowledged with a brusque nod. "Damn right, I saw her. She told me she can't navigate a relationship right now. And to illustrate her point, she asked me to read some—" he clearly worked to hold back an expletive "—some papers by her father's bed."

Frustration rolled off him in waves while Wes's gut sank.

"That...sucks," he settled for saying, knowing how inadequate it was when Ty had been putting all his time into learning how to read.

All the while keeping it secret from Alexis.

Wes had never agreed with that tactic, but he understood it.

"No kidding," Ty muttered dryly, his hand easing off the parking meter as he straightened. "I don't have a clue what those papers said. They could have been discharge forms or a notice that they want to move her dad to hospice. How would I know?"

"You could explain to her—" Wes began gently, but Ty scowled and cut him off.

"No." Anger flashed through his eyes. "I'm not telling the smartest woman I know that if I had a half an hour, I could have sounded out the words on that form. No chance in hell."

Wes saw the fierce determination on his face even as he understood a thing or two about pride. Still, everything inside him rebelled at the thought of Ty's efforts not being enough to win the woman he'd tried so hard to win. If Ty—with his successful baseball career, his willingness to do whatever it took to be with Alexis, his dedication to overcoming the toughest challenge of his life to be a better man—was still found wanting, what the hell kind of chance did Wes have with Emma?

The thought hollowed out his insides while an ambulance careened past them, lights flashing but without the siren.

Wes dropped the matter of Ty's continuing education. "I'll text you after my visit and let you know if I learn anything about her dad's prognosis."

Ty nodded his thanks. "I wish I could have been something to her, but since I'm just in the way, I'm getting the next flight to Palm Beach. Pitchers and catchers are already heading there now. I don't mind setting up house early."

"You can't leave yet." Wes couldn't let Ty fail in his quest to win Alexis. The guy had done everything right, hadn't he? "Not until you tell her how much she means to you."

Ty did a double take. "Says the guy who hasn't risked anything for the woman he wants? And who says I haven't told her?"

"It's not the same. Emma only just came back into my life a week ago—"

"It's exactly the same. Emma means everything to you, and always has, whether you admit it to yourself or not." Ty rubbed the back of his neck, then scrubbed the hand over his face. "In baseball, you have a reputation for not making mistakes. But that's not how real life works. You're going to have to put yourself on the line if you want a shot at her, Wes."

He wanted to argue with him, tell him he didn't know what he was talking about. But how could he when he'd never been depicted so damned accurately? Wes was the Ramsey brother who didn't make mistakes. Growing up in the school of Clint Ramsey had taught him that errors only led to ridicule. So he'd spent countless hours practicing, making his game unassailable. He'd listened to his father lecture Cal and deride Nate, then Wes had made sure not to make those same mistakes.

An outdoor speaker for the hospital PA system crackled to life with an overly loud page for a doctor, cutting short Wes's thoughts.

"I could say the same thing to you." He was ticked off that Ty was just walking away from the woman he was clearly crazy about. Maybe even loved.

Loved? The word stopped him since he'd been comparing Ty's situation to his own.

Did the word apply to how Wes felt about Emma, too?

"I already told her how much I care about her." The pain in the guy's eyes was tough to see. "It didn't make a difference."

This time when Ty shoved past him, Wes didn't try stopping him.

Ty's failure to win Alexis didn't inspire confidence for Wes's pitch to be with Emma, but he had to at least try. His love hadn't enticed her out of Last Stand six years ago, so why would it now when she was so deeply entrenched in her job and the community? For the life of him, he couldn't think of what more he had to offer a woman who'd always made it clear she didn't want to spend her life on the road.

But unlike Ty, he wasn't willing to quit until he'd tried everything he could think of to make her change her mind.

***

EMMA BALANCED TWO to-go cups of coffee from the cafeteria as she approached the door to Mr. Harper's room. A nurse pushing a vitals machine angled her way out, so Emma was able to slip through the entrance without having to change her hold on the cups.

A quick scan of the room told her Alexis's father was still sleeping, while Alexis stared out the window at the sun already low on the horizon.

Emma cleared her throat to announce herself. "I brought you some coffee."

Turning, Alexis swiped the sleeve of her pink sweater over her eyes before she took a step closer to reach for it. Underneath the sweater, she wore a pair of purple scrubs. She must have had physical therapy appointments today before her dad's fall. "Thank you."

"Is everything all right?" Emma asked, hoping she didn't get bad news about her father's condition.

Alexis's eyes were red-rimmed. She sniffed before taking a sip of the coffee, the scent of hazelnut filling the room. "Honestly? I don't know," she said quietly before glancing up again. "Where's Josie?"

"She returned to the farm to take care of the dogs. We left in a hurry this morning." Emma set her own cup on a narrow table underneath the whiteboard where nurses wrote notes about the patient in dry-erase marker. "Is it your dad? Are they worried about him?"

"No. I mean, he's not out of the woods yet, but at least he's stable." Alexis took another quick gulp of her drink before she set the cup on the deep windowsill, then leaned into the ledge herself to take a seat. The sheer yellow curtain fluttered near her thigh as she settled herself. "I'm just trying to make sense of something Ty said when he was here."

"Did he leave already?" Emma was surprised by that since she knew how much Ty wanted to make things work with Alexis. She'd been a big part of what had inspired his efforts with the reading program.

"Yes. Just a couple of minutes ago." Alexis sounded strained. Her gaze went to her father's bedside briefly, as if she needed to make sure he was still comfortable. "And maybe it's my own fault he's not here. He tried to offer me help, and I was flustered because all I really needed was having him here, but I got worried about not being able to be in a relationship."

Emma frowned as she hurried over to the wide ledge in front of the window to sit by her friend. Worry pulled at her. "Why? I thought you would give Ty a chance. He's an incredible guy, and he's crazy about you."

"I'm not so sure anymore." She reached to wind her long ponytail around her fist, then let go of the blond strands, watching them spill over her hand. "I got the weirdest vibe off him today when I showed him the Do Not Resuscitate order the nurse wants me to fill out for my father."

"I'm sorry your dad is at the point where you have to think about that." Emma tugged her friend into a hug, rubbing her shoulder for a moment before she straightened, a sinking feeling taking hold of her.

What did Alexis mean that she *showed* Ty the order? Had he known what he was looking at?

"Thank you." She sniffled and tugged two tissues out of a cardboard box on the rolling cart near her dad's bed. "I know I was using my dad's health as an excuse, but it is scary right now, and I thought maybe seeing those stark words on paper, Ty would better understand what I'm going through—"

"Oh, Alexis," Emma murmured before she could stop herself.

"What?" She blinked up at Emma, hurt and frustration etched in her pretty face. "You didn't see how he looked at it."

Emma's hopes sank. She ached for Alexis, but she could only imagine how Ty was feeling right now. Still, no matter how much Ty's secret was tearing them apart, it wasn't hers to tell.

To cover her unease, she looked over at the hospital bed, where Mr. Harper appeared smaller than when she'd seen him at the wildflower farm a few weeks ago. She remembered that his wife—Alexis and Keely's mom—had abandoned the family long ago. Jimmy Harper had never found another love.

A fact that underscored what a rare and precious gift it was to experience a romance. Was it a mistake not to reach out and take a chance on love when it was so very close? The industrial clock on the wall over the bed hummed in the quiet room.

"It was hard for Keely to go with Nate when he wanted her to leave Last Stand," Emma reminded herself as much as she reminded Alexis. Keely had been the center of the Harper family ever since her father had started drinking, and she'd taken pride and pleasure in helping Alexis through school by starting Windy Meadows Wildflowers. Keely had also cared for her dad as liver damage caught up to him, and it had been tough for her to walk away from the role she'd played in the family to live her own life.

"I remember," Alexis retorted with more sharpness than Emma expected. She pushed to her feet and walked over to the dry-erase board, fiddling with the markers. "I practically had to twist her arm to hand over the reins with Dad and the farm."

"She didn't expect you to keep the farm going, you know." Emma had thought of Keely often this week, missing her friend and longing for her advice since she'd walked the same path Emma was contemplating now.

Sort of. Was she really considering the possibility of leaving Last Stand? Her night with Wes had thrown her feelings into a tumult.

"But the wildflowers are beautiful," Alexis said wistfully. She uncapped a green marker and drew a row of grass along the bottom of the board. "I never thought our run-down farm would be pretty again, but somehow Keely managed it. I want to invest in her work, the same way she invested in me."

The sweet sentiment made Emma wish for a sister. Although, on the heels of that thought, she felt a pang about not seeing her mother in over a year. Maybe she should have tried harder to get out to the West Coast over spring break.

"You know she'd want you to invest in your love life too though. Look how happy Nate Ramsey has made her." Emma slid off the window ledge and returned to her coffee cup, picking it up to take a sip.

"What about you, Emma?" Alexis uncapped the blue

marker and fixed her with a steady gaze. "Are you putting any effort into your love life?"

"I've got my dates all lined up," she retorted weakly. "Remember my matches?"

Truth was she never wanted to be on a dating app again in her life. Especially when Wes was the only guy to ever completely captivate her.

"All I'm saying is," Alexis continued, sketching bluebonnets scattered through the grass she'd drawn "maybe I'll find my courage when you find yours."

Emma was silent for a long moment, her stomach in knots at the thought of losing Wes next weekend.

She didn't realize Alexis was staring at her until her friend spoke again.

"It's easier to give the advice than to take it, isn't it?"

No freaking kidding.

She would never know what answer she would have made to that question though, because there was a soft rap at the door followed by a swish. Wes Ramsey stood framed in the entrance, his broad shoulders taking up too much space—both in the room and in her heart.

The stuttering beat of her pulse told her that she was too far gone on this man already.

She watched as he offered sympathetic words to Alexis, his kindness and thoughtfulness evident in his presence as much as the bright bouquet of amaryllis he'd brought for the room. Emma found herself wanting to tuck herself under his arm and lay her cheek on his chest. She wanted to fall asleep in his arms for the second night in a row.

There'd be time enough to miss him when he left for Arizona next week. Why squander these last days when they could be together now?

He turned to her several minutes later. "Would you like a ride home, Emma?"

Her attention went to Alexis who raised a questioning eyebrow at her. She hadn't forgotten their talk. Or the instruction to find her courage.

Feeling like she was on the edge of a precipice, she stole a shaky breath and nodded.

"Yes. That would be great."

"YOU OKAY?" WES asked as he drove Emma back to her house from the hospital late that afternoon. She'd seemed fidgety at the hospital, tense and nervous. Which was to be expected given the heartache that her friend was going through. But he wondered if there was more to it. They hadn't gotten to speak privately since their heated night together, and he hoped like hell she didn't have any regrets. "I feel bad you had to get a ride from Josie this morning. I would have taken you to the hospital if I'd known."

Stopping the pickup truck at an intersection, he peered at her, allowing his gaze to wander over her profile. Her features were so familiar to him. How many times had they driven around town this way when they were dating, with her teasing touches along his arm while he sought someplace deserted where they could kiss for as long as they wanted?

Even then, their time together had felt stolen. His from his father's expectations that he practice every second he wasn't in school or on the field with his team. Hers from her mother's need to have Emma close by to fix the daily disasters that Adeline had never been good at handling—appliances not working, electricity shut off because she forgot to pay a bill, dramas with coworkers. Looking back, Wes wondered when Emma's mom had decided that her teenager was more capable at navigating life than her.

But it's not like Wes and Emma had suddenly found more time to be together now that they were adults. He could hardly take a breath without thinking about what life would be like once he left for spring training. Would he convince her to keep seeing him somehow? There had to be creative ways they could be together during his season without her having to give up the whole life she'd built here.

"I know. But Josie didn't mind, and I figured you and Cal could use the time to talk to your grandfather." She smoothed her hand over the logo on his old baseball jersey—something she must have pulled out of his drawer this morning. It looked far better on her. "But I've been thinking about Ty and Alexis, hoping they'd work things out. Have you spoken to Ty?"

The sky turned darker as the sun disappeared on the horizon, just a splash of golden light remaining as they neared her home.

"I saw him on my way into the hospital." He wished like hell that story had a better outcome, because if Ty couldn't convince risk-taking Alexis Harper to take a chance on life with a successful ballplayer, why did Wes think he'd persuade practical Emma to leave the only place that had ever felt like home to her? "He's getting a flight for Palm Beach first thing in the morning."

"He can't do that." Emma bent to retrieve her purse on the floor, picking up the leather bag and withdrawing her phone. Her auburn hair spilled onto her shoulder, making him want to stroke his fingers through it. "I'm going to text him. Bad enough he wants to walk away from Alexis, but he can't just quit his reading program when he's come so far. I think he's at a crucial stage for an educational breakthrough."

"Really?" He turned onto Emma's street, ready to be alone with her. Needing to have her in his arms again after the incredible time they'd spent together at his place the night before. He'd been reliving it all day long. "I didn't know it worked like that."

She paused in her scroll through the contacts on her screen. "Honestly? I don't know either. But he was so immersed and motivated that it can't hurt for me to push him to stick with it. And if it gives him time to come to his senses and be honest with Alexis—"

"You think he should tell her?" Wes asked, wondering how she always seemed to see things so clearly—the answers in black and white for her. Kind of like his brother, Cal.

When Emma had a plan, she followed through. That's how he knew for damned sure that if he didn't convince her to give their relationship another chance this year, she'd use her dating app to work through the rest of her list of eligible bachelors. She'd be hitched before the year was out. And the idea of her with someone else had him grinding his teeth so hard his jaw ached.

Why couldn't she see they were right for each other?

"Yes," she answered after a moment, glancing out the window at a couple walking their dog down her street. "What woman wouldn't be flattered to learn a man was devoting all his time to becoming the best possible version of himself for *her* sake?" Her blue eyes darted his way. "I think it's romantic."

The wistfulness in her voice punched him in the gut, making him want to be the man who inspired that tone.

"If I thought there was any chance that learning a second language would convince you to give me a chance, I'd already be taking lessons." His grip tightened on the steering wheel.

She laughed softly. "Since you've never failed at anything, you'd probably be fluent before the season ended."

He pulled into her driveway and shut off the ignition, hoping she'd invite him in. Needing another night with her to remind her what they could be like together. Not just one night. But every night.

"Fluency wouldn't be the motivation though. You're the goal, Emma." He threaded his fingers through hers and then lifted her hand to his lips to kiss the back.

Her skin smelled of ginger and grapefruit, a spicy citrus that belonged only to her. He wanted to taste her everywhere.

Starting with her lips, now parted in surprise or pleasure. He leaned closer over the center console, breathing her in, when the screen door slammed on her house.

He straightened up in time to see Adeline Garcia on Emma's front porch, dressed in a bright green sweater and matching polka-dot dress, one arm raised in delighted greeting.

"Surprise, honey!" she called, rushing toward the truck, her auburn curls bobbing with her steps. "Guess who found a discount airfare from Los Angeles?"

Emma's grip tightened on his. "I can't believe she's here."

Wes's stomach sank as he saw his opportunity to be with Emma tonight fade.

Before he even opened the truck door, Adeline pressed a rusted, dirt-covered box against the passenger-side window.

"My baby girl still keeps the hide-a-key in the marigolds, just like her mama taught her," her mother drawled. "Now come on in and let's get some dinner."

Chapter Twelve

E MMA FOLDED HALF-HEARTED origami shapes with her dinner napkin, all the while waiting for Wes to bail on this date-gone-wrong, complete with her wacky mother as chaperone.

She got halfway through making a swan that started to look more like a pregnant duck, then she smoothed the napkin flat again while her mother spun a story of her first Los Angeles audition that had been "just for kicks." Emma remembered her mother liked to try everything unique about each geographical area she lived in, so it added up with her usual travel goals to give acting a try while she was close to Hollywood.

But how could Wes nod and smile at her mom's liberally embroidered tall tale when sharing this meal meant they were missing out on their last days together before he left for spring training? The memory of his kiss on the back of her hand still hummed on her skin. She wouldn't have blamed him if he fired up his truck and rolled out the first available excuse to avoid an uncomfortable meal with her mom. But instead, he'd worked beside her, helping her prepare chicken and biscuits for a quick meal while Adeline sat at the kitchen island, describing all of the sights she'd seen on the Uber ride from the Houston airport to Last Stand.

And despite the frustration of having her time with Wes interrupted so unexpectedly, Emma couldn't deny that it had been nice to have him working alongside her, companionably chopping veggies, pouring drinks and setting the table. But most of all, he'd held up the conversation and put Emma more at ease.

Still, she kept waiting for him to push back from the small kitchen table and return to the Ramsey family farmhouse where he had his own life to organize before stepping on a flight to Arizona. She glanced sideways at him now, remembering how it had felt to be underneath him the night before, all that muscle at her fingertips while he made her feel incredible.

Her fingers slid absently along the paper she'd been folding, and she wished she was touching him instead.

"Oh, look at you go, Emma." Her mother's voice pulled her from her thoughts. "You were always good at the crane. I think I can only remember how to make the frog."

Adeline reached for her own paper napkin and smoothed it out on her placemat next to her empty plate. Emma peered from her folded creation over to her mom's, surprised her mother had recognized what she was doing.

Wes frowned as he reached for a pewter water pitcher and poured himself another glass. "Cranes? Frogs? I think I missed something in this conversation."

Adeline laughed, her fingers moving nimbly over the stiff

paper napkin. "Emma's trying hard not to say that she wants to wring my neck for showing up unannounced, so she's taking out her stress on perfectly folded paper art, making order out of chaos like she does best."

Wes's eyebrows went up, but he remained silent, no doubt wishing he'd escaped this meal earlier.

For her part, Emma drew up short. She didn't think she'd given any indication of her frustration, but her mother identified it so succinctly that Emma wondered if Adeline had always been so perceptive.

"I don't want to wring your neck, Mom," Emma assured her now, shoving aside the paper creation and standing to clear the plates. "I'm glad to see you."

"But?" Adeline asked, spinning her napkin in a half circle to make more folds.

The soft swish of the overhead fan swirling in the next room had never sounded so loud as in the quiet that followed.

"There's no *but*," Emma insisted, knowing it had to have been expensive for her mother to purchase a last-minute plane ticket. There had been a time when Adeline had told her she'd never return to Texas after being stuck there all through Emma's high school years. "It's good to see you, Mom. Really. I just wish I could have been home when you arrived. If I'd known you were coming I could have had a better welcome for you."

She dumped her dishes in the kitchen sink and then returned to the table for more. Wes shot to his feet, and started to clear the leftovers, working wordlessly beside her.

It wasn't her mom's fault that Emma had hoped to spend more time with Wes before his imminent departure. Things felt unsettled between them. Unfinished. Yet, how could it be otherwise with both of them so dug in on opposing plans for the future?

"Emma." Adeline sat back in her chair, crossing her slender arms over her bright green sweater. "I came all this way to be a help to you, so there's no sense trying to hide from me whatever you're upset about."

Emma shook her head, confused but not surprised that her mother would have elaborate motives Emma wasn't aware of. Once, Adeline had campaigned the Creekbend High School drama teacher to give Emma a lead role in the school play even though Emma had wanted to paint scenery. Another time, during the summer they'd lived in a tiny lighthouse off the coast of Maine, Adeline had insisted Emma walk with a book on her head for an entire summer to give her a more graceful walk. Although, to her mom's credit, it had been Adeline's idea for them to take paperfolding classes at a community center when they'd lived in a town outside of Portland, Oregon. They'd ended up decorating their barren apartment with a paper chain of origami cranes.

Adeline had taken particular pleasure from folding a series of birds from pink and yellow "past due" notices, telling Emma it was the best possible use for the paper. Which was fine until they'd spent two weeks without power in the little apartment they'd been renting.

"You came to help me?" Emma ventured, brushing shoulders with Wes as he strode past her to store leftovers in the refrigerator. "With what, exactly?"

Adeline tilted her head sideways and cast a meaningful glance at Wes while his back was turned. "You *know*. That problem you've been trying to fix. With your dating life."

Emma searched her brain to recall what she could have said to her mom on the phone the last time they'd talked. She sure hadn't brought up Wes. But now that she thought back to the conversation, she remembered complaining about the lack of dating options in Last Stand. She'd been so disheartened to match with a handful of guys that she never would have chosen for herself.

"I already took care of that," Emma tried to tell her quietly, not wanting to discuss this in front of Wes.

She watched him rinse plates and arrange them in her dishwasher, one arm braced on the counter in a way that made his muscles flex.

Had something as mundane as triceps ever thoroughly captivated her before? Then again, on Wes Ramsey, "mundane" and "triceps" had nothing to do with one another.

"She's going to date me instead, Adeline," Wes called over his shoulder. He'd always used her first name, the way her mother had insisted with Emma's friends. "It's all settled."

Adeline's hazel eyes met Emma's, a pleased smile curving her lips even as Emma wondered what Wes was doing to get her mother's hopes up.

Or maybe it was her own hopes that she couldn't bear to see raised, only to be dashed down the road when Wes realized he didn't want a woman who craved roots. A woman who had to have them after spending half her life on the road.

"Is that true, Emma?" Adeline asked, a wicked gleam lighting her gaze as she narrowed her eyes. Tilting her head to study Emma, her mother's red curls bounced sideways. "Are you finally going to stop using the idea of home as an excuse to tether yourself to Last Stand? This town has been like a lead weight chained to your ankle, when all you need to do is set yourself free."

For a moment there was no sound save the overhead fan. Wes had stopped loading the dishwasher as he turned to watch her too. Did he agree with her mother?

Right now, she didn't have any desire to find out. She simply turned on her heel and walked out of the kitchen, shoving through the screen door to escape into the night air.

WES WATCHED EMMA leave, frustrated as hell that her mother had to push her every last button. Especially when he had thought he was making headway with her.

How many more times would he stare after Emma Garcia as she walked away from him?

Drying his hands on a towel next to the sink, he prepared to go after her. But first, he needed to clear the air with Adeline.

"Sorry, Wes," she said softly, picking idly at the full skirt of her polka-dot dress as she sat back from the kitchen table. "It's a flaw of mine that I don't always recognize people's boundaries. Especially my daughter's."

Her insight surprised him. He sensed a maturity in her that he didn't remember from the years she'd lived here with Emma.

"You've changed," he observed out loud before he could stop himself.

She peered up at him in surprise. "Do you think so?"

"I do. You seem happier. More settled."

"I met someone," she confided, the old coyness returning in a flirtatious gesture. But, as if catching herself, she stopped midstream, relaxing her shoulders and smiling. "That's half the reason I made this trip. I'm so excited about him I wanted to tell Emma all about him."

"Really?" He wanted to find Emma and pull her into his arms, but he hated to leave her mom now when she seemed to be making an effort to smooth things over with her daughter. "You should have brought him with you. I'm sure Emma would like to meet him."

"I did bring him, actually." Adeline rested her elbows on the table to lean forward, as if sharing a secret. "I could have never made the drive all by myself. Bernard insisted on staying at a hotel nearby until I figure out a way to tell Emma."

Wes considered how much more smoothly dinner might have gone if Adeline had simply brought the guy with her. Emma surely would have been pleased to have her mother's attention deflected away from her. As for Wes's part, he would have known there was hope in sight for being alone with Emma eventually.

The thought of her wandering around alone in the dark now made him edgy. He wanted a future with her, not all this uncertainty. He wanted to see her smile and make her happy. He just wished he had a clue how to go about it.

"Emma's going to be thrilled for you," he assured her mom. "I know she will. But first, I'm going to talk to her."

Adeline nodded as she pulled her phone out from a pocket in her sweater. "Okay. I'll text Bernard and let him know how it's going."

Wed nodded, leaving her to it. But on his way out the door, he couldn't help but turn back to say, "She's happy here, Adeline. Last Stand doesn't feel like a chain to her. It's her home."

If he wasn't so sure of that, his task in convincing her to come with him wouldn't feel so insurmountable. As it was, he wasn't certain that being with him would be enough to woo her away from all the things that she loved about the life she'd built for herself here.

Adeline pursed her lips, not looking convinced. "She used to love a new adventure as much as me. I'm not sure what happened. But you're going to need good luck to get her to change her mind."

On that point, they were in perfect agreement.

He grabbed a sweatshirt from his truck before he circled around to the back of the house. Wes found Emma at the edge of the trees. He smiled to remember standing there in days gone by, looking at her window and wondering if he could get away with throwing a pebble at the casement without her mother hearing.

She turned before he got too close. She must have heard his footfall through the damp grass.

"I thought you might be cold." Wes covered her shoulders with the sweatshirt, sweeping her silky hair out from under the cotton fabric so it didn't pull. The scent of her shampoo teased his nose and he couldn't resist leaning closer to brush a kiss over the softness. "How are you doing?"

"Honestly? I could probably benefit from your arms around me." She turned to face him, her expression uncertain as a sudden breeze kicked up to blow through her hair, brushing it along her cheek.

"With pleasure." He hauled her against him, tucking her close. "I've been wanting to do this all day."

For that matter, he wanted her. Not just to hold her or to bring into his bed, although he'd never deny he wanted those things too. All the time.

But he wanted *her*—the giving, sweet nature of Emma Garcia—to be a part of his life. He wanted to talk to her every night and ask her how her day went. Ask her for advice on programs at a possible farm camp. Cook meals with her. Care for her whenever she'd let him.

After a long moment, Emma eased back. He kept his hands on her waist though, liking the feel of her through the sweatshirt. Her narrow waist and the soft curve of her hips. He smoothed over them both with his palms, backing her against the trunk of a cedar elm.

"I'm not tethered to Last Stand." There was a quiet anger in her words, forcing him to recall her mother's accusation that had sent Emma from the house. "It's not a character defect that I happen to enjoy a sense of home."

The strong emotion behind the words troubled him, especially when he'd been building toward asking her to spend time with him in San Francisco this season.

"I know that." He tipped his forehead to hers, wishing he could understand her better. What could he say to entice her away from her home, her job, and her friends? "And for what it's worth, I think your mother knows too."

Emma's brow furrowed. She stepped away from the tree, out from under his touch to pace toward the grass at the edge of the lawn.

"What makes you say that? She very deliberately antagonized me back there with her charged language that I'm *chained* here." Emma shook her head, the auburn strands dimmed in the moonlight.

An owl hooted in the distance.

Wes flexed his fingers, already missing the feel of her. This day had veered further and further off course ever since he left Emma's side for his pre-dawn run. He wished he'd never left the bed.

"Right." He'd certainly spent enough time around his own manipulative father to understand the way people leveraged words to create a reaction. Clint Ramsey was a master of subtle belittling. "But she didn't do that because she thinks you're really chained here. She just said it to get a rise out of you. Like if she needles you enough you'll argue with her and prove her wrong."

"So I can start moving around the country every eight months again, like she used to?" Emma folded her arms over her chest as if suppressing a shiver. She paced faster around the tree, her words speeding up. Sounding agitated. "Do you know she used to shake me awake in the middle of the night to tell me it was time to leave? I couldn't pack anything but a toothbrush so we could give a landlord the slip."

Wes hadn't known that. But he couldn't tell Emma as much because she continued speaking, pacing faster.

"Is it any wonder I enjoy waking up in the same bed every day? It's a privilege I don't take for granted. She felt so suffocated by having to stay here during high school that she'd come up with these weird, spur-of-the-moment day trips just to scratch the travel itch. And I went with her every time, knowing full well it was my fault that it was smothering her free spirit to have to stay in one place for four whole years."

"Is that why you went to Mexico at midnight that one time?" Wes's understanding of her upbringing shifted to accommodate this new picture.

"My mom needed adventure. Freedom. As if *I* was the

tether and the damn chain," she murmured.

"I'm sorry, Emma." His heart ached to hear the sadness in his voice. No doubt Adeline had never been subtle. And, remembering her words in the kitchen after Emma left, she didn't understand people's boundaries. But he did. At least, he understood Emma's. Didn't that mean there was a chance that traveling with him would be different from when she'd been on the road with her mom? "You definitely aren't a chain. If I had a choice, I'd always choose being near you."

Her gaze flickered up to his as she lifted her head. "What—" She paused. Licked her lips. "What do you mean?"

He propped an arm against the cedar elm, needing a stable foundation for what he was going to propose.

"I understand why you've wanted to be in Last Stand. It's a great home." Hell, he loved it here. He would retire here. "But if you left now—with me—it wouldn't be for the sake of adventure or freedom. It would just be so we could be together as much as we want to be." He dug deeper, knowing she deserved more than that. "I want to be with you, Emma. Not just in the off-season. All the time."

Her jaw fell open for a moment. Then snapped shut again. She blinked twice before she spoke carefully.

"I've built a life here that I'm proud of." She tucked deeper into the sweatshirt as if the temperature had dropped. "I love my job. I really understand the kids I teach since I remember vividly how it felt to be a teen. My students are the same age I was when I came to Last Stand."

That hadn't occurred to him before, but it made sense that she would have a lot of memories of that time. But the fact that the job meant so much to her wasn't so easy to overcome.

"You could teach online," he suggested, attacking the problem to find the right answer. "Or be a tutor. You're so good with Ty. Working one on one with students comes naturally to you."

She nibbled on her lower lip for so long he knew he must have said something wrong. "You know how you've worked your whole life to be in the majors?"

He nodded.

"What if I said that you're so good at baseball you should coach Little League instead?" There was an edge to her voice.

"Emma, that's not fair." Frustration gnawed at him. "You know your field better than I do. You tell me what you could do on the road to still live your dreams. There must be something."

When she didn't answer right away another thought occurred to him. One that threatened to take the wind out of his sails.

"Unless you don't want to be with me?" he pressed. The ground seemed to tilt beneath him at the thought. At the idea he hadn't even considered after the way they'd been together the night before. "Maybe I should have started there and worried about how to manage it afterward." He took a deep breath and tried again. "So tell me this, Emma. If we didn't have our jobs or distance to concern ourselves with, would you want to keep dating me?"

"We do though," she retorted, a cool note in her voice, matching the ice in her eyes. "You can't separate who we are from what we do. We've both worked hard to get where we are."

The frustration he'd been feeling earlier snowballed into something bigger. Colder. It hurt that she hadn't answered his question. Hurt like hell, if he was being honest.

"Any chance you're digging your heels in about this tonight because your mother showed up in town and got you fired up about it all over again?"

He knew it was the exact wrong thing to say the moment he'd said it, but he couldn't call the words back now. It was too late on so many levels.

"No." The brittle word was spoken with emphasis. "There's no chance of that. Maybe I just don't want to pack up all my dreams and put them on a shelf in favor of yours, Wes. I might not earn a million-dollar paycheck, but I'm good at what I do, and kids count on me." Her shrug was stiff. "For me, that's enough to make me want to stay."

He needed a rewind button to take back the direction of this conversation. But, since there was no such thing, he simply had to watch the woman he loved walk away from him.

Again. This time for good.

Chapter Thirteen

S ITTING ALONE ON the front porch of the Harper farm
late that night, Alexis stared up at the stars while she
turned her cell phone over and over in her hands. She took
comfort from the wide-open spaces all around her, even on
the toughest night of her life. Her father wasn't doing well.
And she'd screwed things up with the hot baseball player
she'd fallen for, sending him running when she needed him
most.

Not that she had any right to need Ty now. She didn't
blame him for leaving.

She'd changed into sweats and an old T-shirt from her
college days when she'd returned from the hospital a couple
of hours ago. Her dad was stable for tonight, and his primary
physician had told Alexis she could bring him home later in
the week if she wanted. When he'd let that last part—the "if
she wanted"—linger a moment, as if waiting for her to
understand his meaning. And when Alexis had inquired what
he thought was best for her dad, the doctor admitted a care
facility might be a better option for him at this point. Ever
since then, she'd been wrestling with herself. The whole
reason she'd wanted to spend more time in Last Stand was to

be with her dad in his final months.

And she had.

But in the six months since she'd moved home, she'd seen him decline. He couldn't handle the stairs in the house anymore, and just thinking about him taking that tumble this morning made her shudder. She couldn't justify keeping him home if his environment had become a danger to him.

But she wouldn't make the decision without first calling her sister. Alexis watched a shooting star streak across the sky, then gave in and hit the phone icon near her sister's name on the screen. Before the device even indicated it was ringing on her end, Keely's voice was right there in her ear.

"Hey," Keely said softly. There was a shuffling noise in the background as if her sister was moving around. Maybe getting more comfortable or seeking a quiet spot to talk. "I've been hoping you'd call. How's Dad doing?"

The sense of failure weighed heavy on Alexis's shoulders. "Not great." In a rush, she shared everything the doctor had told her, along with her guilt that their father had fallen down the stairs on her watch. "So he's stable from the fall, but his overall health is declining faster every day."

She hated sharing all fears with her sister, remembering the way Keely had borne the brunt of the tough days at home while Alexis pursued her degree and then her career. Keely had never complained. She'd just worked harder to keep all the balls in the air that she'd juggled for years.

"Alexis, you can't keep him at home," Keely told her flatly. "You've had six months with him, but now he needs more care. Do what the doctor is telling you and get Dad set up someplace where he'll be comfortable."

"I know you're right." Alexis squeezed the phone tighter, wishing Ty were with her to hold her. Tell her things would be okay. But she'd been too selfish with him for too long, not offering him enough in return because she was scared she'd mess things up when she was going through the most stressful time of her life. Since when did love schedule itself into a planner? It just happened. "But it still feels so wrong to foist off Dad's care on strangers."

"I understand." Keely huffed out a windy sigh, her voice so close it could almost be coming from the rocking chair beside Alexis. "You're talking to the woman who delayed her life for years in order to be indispensable to everyone else. But I'm telling you from hard-won experience that it's a mistake. Don't put your own life on hold for a man who hurt us too many times to count over the years. He wouldn't want you to, Alexis."

The wind kicked up around the porch, blowing the fringe of the chenille throw on her lap, flipping over a corner of it.

Her sister's words echoed something Emma had told her at the hospital earlier. *You know she'd want you to invest in your love life too.*

Except she'd lost that chance now. Ty had packed his suitcase the night before. She'd only delayed his departure for spring break with the impromptu drive around Last Stand checking out make-out spots. The memory of it made her dizzy with happiness, if only it wasn't tinged by the bitter aftermath of today.

"Alexis? You still there?" Keely asked after a long moment.

"Yes." She shouldn't be feeling sorry for herself when she'd caused all of this unhappiness by not grabbing hold of Ty with both hands. Needing to deflect any questions about her, she asked her sister, "How's Nate?"

The dreamy sigh had become a predictable response, but it made Alexis smile to hear. She didn't begrudge her sister a second of her well-deserved romance, but it still hurt to hear about it right now.

"Amazing, actually." The smile in Keely's voice was unmistakable. "I'm getting excited to fly to Arizona with him for spring training. I hope you go to Palm Beach to see a few of Ty's games. He's been so good to you, making a long-distance romance work between Last Stand and Houston."

"I know." Alexis blinked up at the stars, trying to restrain a tear from falling at the thought of how patient Ty had been as she settled into life here. "He's been the best."

She didn't hear what her sister said in response though, as the rumble of an engine in the distance grew louder. As if it was coming closer.

Not just any engine either. The smooth and powerful growl wasn't the kind of noise a tractor made. It had the distinctive sound of Ty's super-size pickup truck.

"Keely, can I call you back?" Alexis said just as the jacked-up headlights came into view on the long driveway leading to her house.

Alexis's heart revved faster than the vehicle headed her way. Disconnecting with her sister, she tossed her phone on the rocker cushion and stepped down into the gravel driveway as Ty pulled up in the shiny black Ford with almost as much swagger as the man himself.

Almost.

Her breath caught as he levered open the door and stepped down to the gravel driveway. She wanted to throw herself at him, to explain how wrong she'd been to put off happiness while she worked nonstop to somehow pay her sister back for all the years Keely had managed at home.

But something in Ty's cool gaze stopped her. He strode closer, his well-worn jeans hugging his thighs. A thin cotton tee skimmed his strong upper body the way she wanted to with her fingers. Alexis dragged her gaze back up to his face, her nerves stretched as he stared at her in the moonlight.

They were only a few feet apart, but it felt like miles.

"I won't keep you." He spoke with brusque efficiency. Like a man in a hurry. "I know you have a lot on your mind, but I had to tell you one more thing before I take off."

Her pulse stuttered.

"You're leaving?" She felt a bubble of hope burst, falling back down to the ground with a splat.

"I booked a flight to Florida for the morning," he confirmed with a nod. His jaw flexed as he studied her.

The air whooshed out of her lungs. She reached a hand to steady herself in a world tipped suddenly sideways, but the porch was too far away. Awkwardly, she took a step back until she was standing closer to the house. She gripped the bottom rail of the balustrade.

"Ty, I wasn't at my best today. I don't blame you for wanting to leave, but—"

"This is tough for me," he interrupted her. And even though she'd long known Ty Lambert had a reputation for bluster, he'd never been that way with her except for the day they'd met. Thinking back to it now, when he'd tried to get out of team-mandated physical therapy appointments with her by coming on to her in the hope she'd refuse to see him—the memory almost made her smile. But Ty was serious now. Really, truly grave as he continued, "Can I just—tell you what I came here to say?"

"Yes." She nodded quickly, steeling herself for the worst. She owed him that much and more. "Sorry."

"Remember when you told me to read that paper next to your father's bed today?"

His words were so unexpected, she whipped her head around to stare at him, to see what she'd missed. She'd thought there'd been a shift in him then, but she hadn't been able to pinpoint it.

"The DNR order. Do Not Resuscitate." Her chest tightened with all the scary things she'd faced today about her father's health. "I remember."

"I couldn't read it." His blue-green eyes bored into her. Fixed. Steady.

"What do you mean?" She tried to follow what he was

saying. Had there been someone in his past with a DNR? "Was it emotionally triggering? I didn't mean to be insensitive—"

"No. I mean I can't read, Alexis. As in, I'm functionally illiterate." He said the words with more venom than she'd ever heard from him. "It wasn't that I didn't want to be supportive. I just had no flipping clue what was on that paper and I—" His hands clenched and unclenched by his sides, but then he seemed to drag in a breath and force himself to go still. "I thought you should know that's why I walked out. I'm done pretending to be something—someone—I'm not. Especially in front of you."

Stunned, she searched for the right words while her mind raced. Moments from their time together circled through her mind, but she couldn't recall any hint of this. Yet she couldn't afford to screw up her response now when he was so obviously angry, and perhaps—sadly—ashamed of something that wasn't his fault.

"Not in a million years would I have ever guessed that, Ty." She couldn't stand for this strong, smart, successful man to feel like he was anything less than those things.

His lips flattened in a look she couldn't decipher. Distaste, maybe. "Put it down to a lifetime of coping mechanisms at work."

He seemed so rigid. Tense. And the way he looked at her now was so different from the way he used to, as if he waited for her to say something disparaging. While she'd made plenty of mistakes with this man, how could he possibly think that she'd be so superficial?

Dismayed at the idea, she straightened from where she held the porch rail, reaching a tentative hand toward him. Gently, she clasped his fingers in hers. His skin was so warm. She missed his touch so much.

"I can't imagine how stressful it's been to accomplish everything you have when you had a proverbial hand tied behind your back all this time." She rubbed her thumb over the back of his hand, willing him to listen to her. To see beyond the times she'd pushed him away, because it didn't have anything to do with him, and everything to do with her own fears. "I'm so sorry you felt like you ever had to pretend in front of me. If anything, knowing the obstacles you've overcome only makes me admire you more."

He shook his head, dismissing her words. "Right. If you go to a dictionary and look up illiterate, you want to guess what some of the synonyms are? And I can do that, thanks to the wonders of Google and text-to-speech. I can ask Alexa for those synonyms."

She hurt to hear the pain in his voice. The undisguised anger. He continued before she could answer.

"Ignorant. Low-browed. Witless. Imbecilic—"

"You are none of those things, Ty." She stepped closer to him, knowing she needed to convince him of that even if she couldn't persuade him to give her one last chance. How he felt was more important than any hurt she might feel. "Not by a long shot. I refuse to let you think those ugly things about yourself when you are, hands-down, the best man I've ever known."

He looked down into her eyes, a thoughtful expression stealing over his face. Considering.

And now that she had his attention, she would make damned sure he heard the rest of what she wanted to say.

"Ty, I'm sorry that you've been weighed down by that. Because everything I know about you proves that you're a caring, giving, incredible guy." She recalled all the times he'd volunteered at Nate Ramsey's baseball camp. How he'd helped her around the farm. Made her smile when she felt like she didn't have anything to smile about. "And only the most witless, imbecilic woman in the world would give you up because she's too ignorant to recognize love when it's right in front of her."

The night wind blew harder, making a howling sound as it wrapped around the house behind her. She gathered her hair in one hand to keep it from blowing in her face, the other hand still holding Ty's tight.

"Don't say that. You're the smartest woman I've ever met." Ty cupped her face in one broad palm. "I'm so inspired by you, I convinced Emma to teach me to read. It's slow going, but I'm making progress. You make me want to be a better man."

His touch was like balm to her spirit. She closed her eyes, leaning deeper into that caress.

"You make me want to be better, too. Because I haven't been acting like a smart woman. But I'm done being foolish." She hoped it wasn't too late.

He edged back to study her face. "What do you mean?"

Her belly knotted, hoping she could say the words to make things right. To fix the way she'd hurt him. "From now on, I'm only making smart decisions. Starting with asking you to be a part of my life. Not to help me around Last Stand. I want to go see your world and be a part of that, too. Be a help to you, however I can."

"What about your dad? Your business?"

Her eyes burned with the knowledge that her father's short time was dwindling. She would never regret spending these last months with him. "I'll come back to Last Stand to be with Dad on the weekends until…the end." She swallowed hard. "But I can do physical therapy wherever I go. And I'll talk to Keely about hiring a manager for the wildflowers." She tracked Ty's eyes, searching for answers. Knowing he deserved better than her, but wanting him to say yes so much. "I want to be with you, Ty, if you'll still have me."

He wrapped her in his strong arms and held her tight, crushing her to him in the best possible way. She ducked her head into his chest, so grateful for him. For his willingness to listen to her even though she'd been too stubborn. And yes, for his incredibly sexy self.

"Not only will I have you, Alexis Harper." He leaned back to look into her eyes. "I'm going to make you so happy it'll be impossible for you to ever leave me."

Warmth filled her heart along with happiness. Certainty.

"I hope you know you don't need to change anything

about you though, Ty." The truth of her feelings bubbled up inside her, too important to hold back. She knew too well how fast someone you cared about could slip away. "I love you just the way you are."

Ty brushed a kiss over her lips. "I love you more," he breathed the words over her damp mouth. "And I'll make myself better for me, then. I'm seeing progress this time with the program Emma showed me. More than I ever have before."

Alexis nodded, happy for him. And so very thankful for his love that warmed her inside and out.

"I know you'll succeed in this too." She couldn't suppress a smile she felt all the way down to her toes. Full of promise for a future with this incredible man who'd stolen her heart. "For now though, why not come into the house with me and let me show you how happy we can make each other?"

Lifting her off her feet, Ty tucked her against his chest and headed for the door, holding her so tight she knew he'd never let her go.

EMMA STARED OUT the window of the kitchen after breakfast the next morning, unable to find the will to get to her feet and move on with her day. If Adeline hadn't been in town, she would have gladly just stayed in bed and nursed her heartache all day long. The hurt in her chest hadn't eased for a second since things had blown up with Wes.

If anything, it felt deeper. Sharper.

Was it possible for heartache to be fatal? The thought didn't strike her as even the slightest bit melodramatic. Based on her pain level, it seemed like a very real potential side effect.

"Honey, are you done with your breakfast?" Her mother hovered over her shoulder, a dish towel in one hand and a glass container of maple syrup in the other.

Emma had agreed to host Adeline and her new boyfriend Bernard for breakfast this morning only because her mother had been in a hurry for her to meet him.

And he'd seemed nice. A sweetly pleasant, adorably bald improvement over the self-absorbed men she normally dated. If Emma hadn't been so sad about losing Wes, she would have counseled her mother to marry Bernard at the first opportunity since the retired dentist not only doted on Adeline, he also cooked pancakes and cleaned kitchens, even when he should have been the guest in the house.

Emma only vaguely noticed that he had excused himself to do a crossword puzzle in the living room after washing the dishes. Now, while Emma stared out the kitchen window at the spot in the backyard where her romance with Wes had died last night, her mother flitted around the kitchen with restless unease.

"I'm done," Emma answered belatedly, pushing her barely touched food aside. "Bernard is a great cook, Mom."

"You'd hardly know it from looking at your plate," Adeline chastised her as she took the seat closest to Emma. Setting down her towel and the syrup, she clamped a cool hand on Emma's. "Sweetheart, what's wrong? Did you and Wes have a fight?"

"It's over," she said quietly, wishing her aching heart would have gotten the message before now. "I knew it would never work. I don't know how I could have gotten sucked in a second time when we ended things for a good reason the first time."

"You mean *you* ended things the first time." Adeline sighed, kicking back in her chair. She wore a purple shirt dress with big hoop earrings today, her wardrobe as irrepressible as the woman herself. She looked ready to win a disco dance-off. "Hasn't six years taught you that what you feel for Wesley Ramsey is the real deal?"

She hedged, uncomfortable with the idea that Wes was the right guy for her when they'd been as incapable as ever of figuring out a way to be together.

"Six years has taught me that we still want different things." Emma picked at a loose thread on her woven placemat, wondering if he was already in Scottsdale for spring training.

Would he miss her? Did his heart hurt half as much as hers did today? How long would this pain last?

"No, you don't." Adeline tapped a long fingernail on the kitchen table, one beat per word for emphasis. "You both want to be wildly in love with one another. That hasn't changed one whit."

"Mom." She banged her hand on the table for emphasis of her own. "He wants me to give up everything I have here and start over again. I'm not doing that."

In the living room, Bernard turned up the volume slightly on the NPR program he was listening to. He really was a nice man to try to give her and her mom some privacy for this conversation. She wished she'd met him under better circumstances, when her heart wasn't breaking.

"Is that what Wes said to you, Emma? He said, I want you to give up everything and start over?"

"Of course not, but—"

"Of course not," Adeline repeated triumphantly. "Because that's not what he meant. He just wants to be with you, honey. That doesn't mean you need to start over."

She couldn't believe her mother was oversimplifying this, ignoring the practical fact that Emma was committed to teaching. But then again, when hadn't her mother walked through life with rose-colored glasses while the people around her did the hard work?

"What am I going to do for employment?" Emma pressed, wondering if her mother would even recognize this as an obstacle. "Why should I give up a job I worked hard for—"

"Your job will still be around in ten years. In twenty years. Wes's won't, and neither will his career." Her mother reached for her, stroking her hand over Emma's hair. "His opportunity has an expiration date. You know that perfectly well."

She felt a moment of unease wondering if her mom could be right, but then Emma rallied, reminding herself of another important point.

"But does that mean my career is disposable?" She loved working with kids. Losing that would leave a hole in her. "I've built a good life here."

"Just because you leave here to spend time with the man you love doesn't mean you're throwing away what you've built. You can pursue one happiness now, and still circle back to enjoy another in Last Stand down the road." Her mother laid her hand over hers and squeezed it. "Don't make Wes pay for my mistakes, Emma. He's not asking you to leave everything behind. He's just trying to love you."

Was that what she was doing? Carrying over old hurts into her relationship with Wes? She couldn't deny her mother had a point.

Several, even. She glanced out the window at the town she'd thought was her whole world. Now she wondered if she'd been wrong. If home was something more than her narrow definition.

The realization that she might have misjudged her mother—or failed to see that she wasn't the same woman she'd been during Emma's childhood—was just one of the ways she felt rocked by the conversation. For now, the single, biggest thought in her mind was what if her mother was right?

What if Emma was protecting herself to her own detriment? Digging her heels in so hard—hell, Wes had said that very thing to her even though she'd been too stubborn to listen—that she was missing out on the love of a lifetime?

"I should go." Pushing back from the table, she was seized with the urge to find Wes. To tell him she was wrong.

That she didn't want to be with anyone else but him, no matter what that meant.

Adeline smiled, fluffing her curls with all her old affectation and irrepressible good humor. "If you need a ride to Scottsdale, Arizona, honey, maybe Bernard and I can drive back to L.A. so we can drop you off on our way."

Emma hugged her mom hard, the familiar lemon verbena scent reminding her of good times they'd had together. There'd definitely been some that Emma had chosen not to remember. "I love you a lot, Mom, but I'm hoping for both our sakes it doesn't come to that."

Adeline laughed, brushing Emma's hair from her face. "In that case, I'll just cross my fingers you haven't missed Wes."

Her steps fueled by new purpose, Emma snagged her keys off a hook in the wall and hurried out the door. To find her man and claim him—along with their future.

Chapter Fourteen

WES WAS LOADING his pickup truck for the upcoming trip to Arizona when his grandfather approached. Everett was using the quad cane that Cal had bought him earlier in the summer, a device their grandfather had griped about, but it really did help his stability. The four-pronged base made it a little more unwieldy in tight spaces, which was Everett's perpetual excuse for leaving it at home instead of taking it to the farm stand. But between their houses, where the lawns stretched a good forty yards, the cane seemed to come in handy.

Still, it took a lot of willpower for Wes to let the older man come to him when his steps were so labored, but Everett had made it clear to his grandsons that he'd ask for help when he wanted it. Unfortunately, in the time that Wes stood rearranging his suitcases in the truck bed his thoughts went to Emma and how wrong things had gone between them last night. He'd rewritten the conversation a million different ways in his head since then, but even when he imagined more tactful ways to confront her about a future together, the result was still the same. Emma wouldn't give up her life for the sake of his.

Sadly, he understood it, too. It's not like he was sacrificing his career for her. Why should he expect her to do so for him? The question had pulled his thoughts in a lot of surprising directions though. Because, no matter how much he loved baseball, he loved Emma Garcia more. If he had to choose between them, there really was no choice. Emma had a hold of his heart six years ago, and while he'd set her free because it seemed like that's what she'd wanted, he wasn't ready to give her up this time. He had a contract that he needed to honor for one more season, according to his agent, but as soon as he could legally free himself, he'd come home to Last Stand. He just hoped it wouldn't be too late.

"Don't grow old," Everett groused as he reached the back of Wes's pickup truck and seated himself on the open tailgate with a tired sigh.

Wes pushed aside his thoughts of Emma for now, knowing whatever his grandfather had come to say was probably important if he'd broken out the quad cane for the trip. Everett jammed the four prongs into the gravel drive with force.

"The alternative is no good though, Gramp. Should I get you a glass of water or anything?"

"Hell no. If my grandson can do wind sprints for hours in the backyard, I ought to be able to walk across the lawn without it sending me to my sick bed." Everett folded his arms across his thinning chest and glared at Wes.

Wes, for his part, knew better than to argue. He waited for his grandfather to say what was on his mind.

"Going somewhere?" Gramp asked finally, jerking his thumb toward the cargo bed.

"Spring training starts Saturday." Although the whole thing had lost some of its shine now that he'd be going without Emma. He kicked the rear tire closest to where his granddad sat. "I figured I'd take the truck this year. I can bring it to San Francisco with me once the regular season starts."

"It's a little early to be packing up, isn't it?" Everett smoothed his white hair away from his face, his green eyes missing nothing. "What happened to farm camp?"

Wes straightened to look at him. A noisy flock of birds took off from one of the big hickory trees in the front yard, filling the air with squawking.

"Are you seriously considering it?" He'd been afraid his grandfather had just been humoring him when he'd brought up the idea with Cal yesterday.

"I'll do better than consider it." Everett lifted a shaggy eyebrow as he studied Wes. "If you put a ring on your pretty girlfriend's finger, I'll sell you the land you need for it at a discount."

Wes blinked in disbelief—and hope. Cal had tried telling him that their grandfather liked to dabble in matchmaking, but Wes hadn't believed it. "How do you know I have a girlfriend?"

"I have eyes, son. I saw her with you in the yard the other night. And that time at the farm stand too. Just because I get winded walking across the lawn doesn't mean two and two don't still add up to four in the old head." He rapped a knuckle against his temple to illustrate his point. "Besides, everybody knows Emma Garcia loves this town. If you marry her, I'm sure to get at least one grandson back here some-day."

Heart slugging in his chest, Wes clapped his grandfather on the shoulder. "I wish it was that simple. But we're all going to be back here one day, Gramp. Nate and Keely, Cal and Josie. Me." He hated that he couldn't add Emma's name to that list with his yet, but he tried to focus on what was troubling Everett, not what was tearing up Wes's heart today. "We all love Rough Hollow."

"But who's going to take the big house and be a presence here day in and day out?" He pointed to the place where Wes had grown up. "I'm giving your mother my house when I go—"

"That's a long time off," Wes assured himself as much as his grandfather.

"Well I hope so. But I didn't build up the farm business just to see it all sold off. The camp idea is a good one though. And your girlfriend is a teacher. She could help you run it."

The words, while kindly meant, were like salt in the wound of all he couldn't have. Before he could explain to Everett why that wasn't going to happen, however, the sound of tires crunching on gravel reached their ears.

Emma's car was heading toward them.

"That's her, isn't it?" Everett remarked, smoothing his

hair down again. "Don't blow this, Wes. She's a keeper."

Wes's eyes were fixed on her face through the windshield, searching for a clue for why she was here. He refused to get his hopes up though, after the way things ended last night. But it saved him a trip since he'd wanted to make her one last proposition before he left. Just in case there was any chance.

"I'm going to do my best, Gramp. I just don't know if it will be enough." He wanted to wrap her in his arms and not let her go, but he knew that wasn't going to win her over.

"Don't sell yourself short," Everett barked at him, sliding from the tailgate with one hand on the cane. "You've got all Cal's brains and all of Nate's charm, and you're twice as determined as either of them. That's what your grandmother said anyway, God rest her soul, and she was the wisest lady I ever met."

Wes tore his eyes from where Emma parked her car, grateful for his grandfather's words. He could almost hear his grandmother's voice in his head and that made him feel more determined than anything else. He wanted to live up to her faith in him. "Thanks, Gramp."

The older man nodded, his lively gaze already on Emma, but he pitched his voice low for Wes's ears only. "I'll get you started. Sort of like an icebreaker. But I won't stay."

As Emma headed their way, looking prettier than any woman had a right to in pink jeans and a slouchy olive-colored sweater that fell off one shoulder, Wes still couldn't get a read on her. But he wouldn't let that deter him. He was all in. Even if it meant getting his heart broken.

"Hello, Everett." She greeted his grandfather with a polite smile before turning to him. Her smile dimmed a little, but maybe only to his eyes. "Wes."

"Where's your dog today?" Everett asked after saying hello. "I like Sasha."

"I only dog-sit for her every once in a while," Emma explained.

Everett was already pivoting around with his cane, but he winked at Wes when Emma couldn't see. "Well I was just heading back home. Nice to see you, Emma. Try and talk my grandson into staying in town for a little longer, will you?"

Wes would have laughed at the older man's obvious maneuvering, except Wes needed all the help he could get with Emma.

"Can we talk for a minute?" Emma asked Wes as Everett thunked his way across the lawn, cane in hand.

Steeling himself, Wes nodded toward the tailgate. "We can sit here if you want. Or there's shade in back—"

"Here's fine," she assured him, hoisting herself onto the truck bed with ease. She glanced back at his suitcases in the cargo bed behind them. "You're not leaving today, are you?"

Wes settled on the tailgate beside her and braced himself before he dove headfirst into the matter.

"A lot of that depends on you."

EMMA WAS NERVOUS enough about having this talk with Wes without ominous phrases like that one. Wes looked so incredibly handsome in the warm February sunshine, good health and vitality radiating from him as he sat beside her in jeans and an old "Staff" tee from the Rough Hollow farm stand.

"What do you mean?" she asked, knowing no other man in the world was as right for her as the one seated near her.

"For starters, my grandfather promised me I could start my farm camp if I put a ring on your finger."

A startled laugh broke through her nerves. Until she realized Wes wasn't laughing.

"He was joking, of course." Emma toyed with the ribbon her mother had tied around her wrist before breakfast—pale blue velvet and very thin—as a reminder that she could "do anything she set her heart to."

It was a sweetly sentimental thing to say and do, the kind of thing that Emma might have dismissed in the past as one of Adeline's attempts to fix her. But following the talk they'd had after breakfast, Emma had to admit that her mother sometimes saw things more clearly than she did.

"He was perfectly serious. But I think he'll get on board with the farm camp even if you don't say yes."

Emma's attention whipped to Wes's face to see if *he* was teasing her now. But she couldn't see any sign of it in his green eyes as he stared back at her.

Maybe she was misreading this whole thing. Or mishearing.

"Wes." She started over again, feeling like she got off track from what she'd come here to say. "I was upset last night. You were right about that. It had a lot to do with Mom being in town." She'd come a long way toward making peace with her old relationship with her mother, however, she still needed to find a new way to be with her. Forge a better relationship. "But I talked to her at length this morning, and she helped me to see that I really don't want us to be apart."

Wes didn't reply right away. "You and your mom?" he asked finally.

"No." She shook her head, shifting on the truck bed and accidentally bumping his knee with hers. "You and me, Wes." Tentatively, she slid her hand over his forearm. "I don't want to be apart from you."

"That's exactly how I feel," he told her, his green eyes so steady on hers that she knew he was sincere. "That's the point I was trying to make last night. I just did a terrible job of it, and I'm sorry about that."

"No." She took his hand between both of hers and squeezed it. "You have nothing to be sorry for. It was me who was too scared to trust in what we have enough to leave home. But I don't have to leave forever—"

"You don't have to leave at all," Wes told her, a calm sense of purpose coming through in his words. "I was going to come by your house today to tell you that, Emma. You don't need to give up your career for me."

She leaned closer, determined to make him see. "But Wes, I want to—"

"Because I'd give up mine for you." His grin was triumphant. "You're more important to me than baseball."

Stunned, she could only sit there and try to absorb the words that made no sense. She shook her head, more convinced than ever that they were on different wavelengths.

"Ramsey and baseball are practically synonymous." She had to remind herself as much as him. "You can't walk away from a career like that."

"I could though. And I will if that's what it takes to be together. I have the farm. Everett would be thrilled to have us here. You could keep your job."

"No." She laid a finger over his lips, grateful that he hadn't made an offer like that the night before when she might have been foolish enough to take him up on it. "Absolutely not, Wes, although…wow. I'm bowled over to think you would ever consider something like that when you've worked your whole life to reach this level. It's your dream."

Gently, he moved her finger away from his lips, kissing it before he folded her hand against his chest.

"It is." He confirmed it without blinking. Without backing down. His unwavering assurance of this was a little daunting. "Although it was my father's dream before it was mine, and I have other dreams that are mine alone so it's not like I wouldn't achieve other things that are important to me. But *you* are at the center of all of them, Emma. Without you, none of the rest matters."

She couldn't miss the seriousness in his voice. Her heart overflowed at his sweet words. His willingness to walk away from something monumental for her sake. It made her breathless to think he would ever consider it.

She leaned into him, kissing him long and slow to show her how much his offer meant to her. By the time they broke apart, she was a little breathless and all the more in love.

"That is the nicest thing anyone has ever tried to give me." She scooted closer on the tailgate, so their thighs touched from knee to hip. "But all of our other dreams will keep while we chase this one, Wes. We can come back to Last Stand when you're ready, but first, I think you should show the baseball world what you can do."

"Would you travel with me?" He combed his fingers through her hair, making her scalp tingle from his touch.

"I can come for the first week of spring training while I'm on spring break, but I'd have to finish the rest of the school year out." She wouldn't upend her students' lives completely. "But I can be in San Francisco with you by the middle of May if I can convince someone else to monitor my final exams."

Wes plucked her off the tailgate and slid her over to sit on his lap pulling her hip tight to him and kissing her neck. "I could definitely wait for forever to begin if I knew it was going to start at the end of May." He spoke between kisses, his breath warming her skin while his words tempted her with an amazing future.

"Do you really think it will be forever?" She steadied herself with a hand on his shoulder, loving the feel of him. Loving the idea that she could touch him whenever she wanted from now on.

"There is going to be a ring involved, Emma, I guarantee it, and not just because it would make Gramp happy." He edged back enough to look into her eyes, cradling her face in his hands. "Spending forever with you will make me happy. And it will put an end to any and all future dating schemes."

She couldn't stifle a smile, her heart so full that things were working out more beautifully than she could have ever imagined. "I never want to date anyone else ever again, Wes. All my dates are reserved for you, wherever we end up."

"We're going to end up right back here," he promised, returning to the neck kisses that were making her shiver in spite of the warm weather. "The farm camp is happening. Gramp said I should ask you to help me, by the way, since you're a teacher."

"I would seriously love that." She skimmed a hand over his biceps and across his chest, halting to rest over his heart. "I love you, Wes. Thank you for bearing with me while I figured that out."

When she thought about how close she might have come to losing him—to losing this incredible future rolling out in front of them—it sent that same sharp pain into her chest she thought might be the death of her just this morning. She never wanted to take moments like this for granted.

Or Wes. She'd never take this incredible man for granted.

"Emma, I love you like crazy, and I want to spend the rest of my days making you happy." His hand skimmed up the back of her neck, his thumb tracing along her cheek. "That's my main dream."

Heart in her throat, she couldn't answer in words. So she settled for kissing him for a long, long time.

Epilogue

Eight months later

STANDING IN THE kitchen of the old farmhouse in early October, Wes peered out the window into the backyard where the Ramsey clan prepared to celebrate a family reunion. He, Cal, and Nate were all back home, none of their teams having made it to the postseason this year. The disappointment of not being able to extend a solid rookie season had definitely stung at first. But now, Wes appreciated his mother's decision to throw a family picnic for the occasion.

Looking out into the yard where Emma and Keely laughed at Josie's antics as she played tug-of-war with Kungfu the Maltipoo, Wes had to admit there was nowhere in the world he'd rather be today. Especially since they were also celebrating a successful inaugural first session of the farm camp at Rough Hollow. Even now, Everett drove a tractor pulling a hay wagon full of kids around the orchard before their parents picked them up.

"Gramp is in his element out there, isn't he?" Cal observed from over Wes's shoulder. "I think he's having as much fun as the kids."

Everett had recovered some strength through rehab after his injury. And while he'd worked hard to regain muscle, Wes suspected the camp had been good incentive for him to make those efforts. Everett made another turn through the orchard while the wagon full of six- to eight-year-olds waved paper crafts they'd made to look like jack-o-lanterns. They each had coupons to return to the farm stand with their families later in the month to pick out a free pumpkin. Wes knew a whole lot about what the kids did in the themed weekly sessions in fact, because Emma had taken a significant role in making the Rough Hollow Farm Camp educational. She'd joined him for the regular season after school let out in May, and when she wasn't with him, she'd spent her time planning age-appropriate activities for the campers and discussing her ideas with Everett by video call.

Wes would return from off-day workouts to find Emma and his grandfather in deep discussions about raised garden beds where attendees could weed and tend the ingredients for pizza, salads, and peanut butter and jelly sandwiches. Some days Everett would ramble around the farm with his phone to show Emma his progress, and it filled Wes's heart to see those two important people in his life give shape to the camp and form a friendship at the same time.

Of course, being with Emma had been hands-down the best part of the year. She'd surprised him and probably herself too by how much she'd enjoyed the San Francisco area, the city's artsy aesthetic—and great thrift stores—

appealing to the bohemian part of her that time in Last Stand hadn't fully erased. They'd rented a penthouse with incredible views of the bay, thinking they'd find a more permanent house once she had time to explore the area. But Emma liked the apartment as home base for her day trips, even making occasional treks down to Beverly Hills to spend time with Adeline. But anytime Wes was home, she was right there with him, and that had been enough to make the year the best of his life.

Now across the kitchen, Nate whipped a dish towel at Wes to snap him in the shoulder.

"A little help over here?" Nate swept his hand along the butcher-block kitchen countertop where trays laden with pitchers, cups, dishes, and all manner of picnic fare. "One year in the majors doesn't get you out of house chores, bro. A league-leading on base percentage doesn't matter jack to those who knew you when you caught a fly ball in your hat."

Cal laughed as he grabbed a heavy glass pitcher filled with lemonade, the ice cubes and citrus slices on top sprinkled with mint leaves. "Remember how mad Dad was about that?"

Nate launched into a spot-on impression of their father, shaking a finger in their faces. "Boys, this is *baseball*. It isn't a *game*." Nate passed Wes the silver tray full of dishes before he returned to his own voice, his eyes meeting his brother's. "Except I'm having a damn good time with it either way."

"You had a hell of a career year." Wes went through the back door sideways as he juggled the tray and held the screen open for Nate behind him, the scent of grilled chicken already in the air.

Nate had taken the longest to get the call-up to the majors, but after a year and a half on a big-league roster, he was killing it. He'd never been an extra-base hitter, but his RBIs were impressive. When his team needed a hit, Nate delivered.

"I'm glad they're keeping me around for another season." Nate couldn't hide his grin as he followed Wes out onto the grass and toward the pavilion where the rest of the family waited. "Although I'm looking forward to the baseball camp this winter. Don't think I didn't notice you stole my camp idea for the farm."

"Emma pointed that out to me this summer." Wes's gaze went straight to Emma as she walked toward the stopped farm tractor. Two of the camp staff were helping kids off the wagon while vehicles were lined up on the long driveway between the Ramsey houses to pick up their kids. "She said it's no wonder we wanted to 'recreate positive childhood experiences' for ourselves after growing up in the Ramsey full-time training program."

Nate whistled low as they reached the bar under the converted pole barn the family used for outdoor entertaining. "She might have a point. Or it could just be that I have great ideas, and you like to steal them."

Grabbing a dish towel from the sink behind the bar, Wes answered him with a return whip to the shoulder, the slight dampness of the cotton giving the slap an extra kick.

Cal laughed as he arranged the pitchers and food for easy access, but their mom hurried toward them just as Nate was reaching toward Wes to initiate potential retaliation.

"No headlocks today, Nate," Hailey Decker murmured as her hazel gaze moved over the picnic preparations. She tossed her brown ponytail behind her shoulder as she reached behind the bar for a bottle of wine. "Why don't you man the grill for me instead? You could throw a few burgers on now that the chicken is underway."

Nate straightened immediately. The tallest of the three, he easily laid a kiss on the top of her head as he moved toward the fridge to retrieve the meat. "Yes, ma'am."

She beamed up at him before turning her maternal smile on Cal and Wes. "It's so good to have you all home. And your lovely ladies, too."

Outside, the dogs indulged a few happy barks, alerting them to newcomers.

Cal grabbed two beers from an ice tub. "Alexis and Ty just pulled in the drive."

Outside, the last of the campers was off the hay wagon, but Everett and the two camp staff members were still talking to families as they picked up their children. Only a few of the parents' cars remained, however, so the crowd was thinning. Soon it would just be family. Plus Alexis and Ty, who were spending the off-season in Last Stand, too. Alexis's dad had passed six months ago, and she'd spent most of her time in Houston with Ty since then, leaving the wildflower business in the hands of a friend. Ty had finished his literacy program two months ago and had recently celebrated by reading his statement of retirement from baseball from typed notes at a press conference he'd called the week before. Not that anyone but close friends would have noticed the pride he took in reading from those notes. He'd said he wanted to retire to focus on his new job of running Nate's baseball camp in Last Stand year-round. He and Alexis had gotten engaged two weeks ago.

Wes watched as the Harper sisters, Keely and Alexis, hugged one another, two blond heads tipped together. But that was in his peripheral vision since his eyes were focused on Emma as she strode toward him in a yellow-and-white skirt printed with bumblebees. The pleasure he took just from having her in his life every day still seemed like more happiness than any one man deserved. Not that he was complaining. She wore a Rough Hollow Farm Camp T-shirt with an elaborate peach tree logo on it, the roots as detailed as the branches to emphasize the relationship between the soil and the fruit, and the lifecycle of a seed. She'd helped to design it, but her mother had been the one to draw the artwork in a joint effort that had been one of many signs of a healing relationship.

And although the skirt and shirt did all kinds of good things to her curves, Wes couldn't help but notice her pleased expression even more. She edged around the herb garden to meet him by the detached garage.

"Is it too cliché to say we have a lot of happy campers?" She threw her arms around his neck, those delectable curves fitting against him like she was made to be there. "Because based on what I heard from those parents picking up their kids, there will be a lot of good word-of-mouth about the farm camp."

Wes framed her face with his hands before bending to kiss her lips. Once. Twice. She tasted like peaches and honey. Probably from some organic snack the campers made in their cooking class.

"I'm not surprised based on how hard you've worked to give them a great experience." He nuzzled her jaw and nibbled her ear. She tasted good there, too.

She shivered against him in a way that made him want to drag her back to the garage apartment where they were spending the next couple of months while they finished plans for a home of their own in Last Stand.

"I have a good feeling we're going to exceed our financial goals for the camp this year." She couldn't hide the pleasure in her voice. Although he liked to think a little part of that pleasure was from his hands moving down to her shoulders and sliding around her waist. "Not that it's just about the money—"

"You're giving those kids a great experience," he assured her, since Emma had struggled with educating children in a for-profit environment. "And don't forget how much we've earmarked for scholarships to get more kids here to experience what you and Everett are building."

He knew the way to her heart was through those scholarships. He'd talked his brothers into funding a whole session in the winter for teacher-recommended candidates who could benefit from the farm's offerings. But in the future, they hoped to give a percentage of scholarships based on profits.

"Thank you for giving me a way to keep teaching." She tipped her forehead to his shoulder while he pulled her closer.

"Thank you for giving my grandfather a way to enjoy the farm again. He didn't have a single protest about the manager we brought in to oversee the daily operations of the orchards and farm stand." Wes had been quick to see the benefit of the farm camp for its high return potential on a small piece of their land, but also for the outlet it gave Everett who still needed to feel connected to his land.

It turned out his grandfather was every bit as passionate about teaching sustainability and conservation to kids as Emma, and he'd gladly left the farm management to new staff so he could be involved with the camp.

"The kids adore him." Emma pulled away from him to look back toward the hay wagon and tractor where Everett was shaking hands with the last remaining camper's father. "But we should go congratulate Ty and Alexis on their engagement. According to Keely the ring is a 'must-see.'"

Wes let himself be pulled along to congratulate his friend, knowing all the while he had a ring of his own tucked in his luggage in the garage apartment. And while it wasn't what most people would think of as a "must-see" since it was rose quartz surrounded by diamonds instead of the traditional diamond, it had a storied, happy history behind it that he was sure would appeal to her quirky sense of style.

That was for another day, since he wanted to propose to the woman he loved by Hickory Creek where they had so many shared good memories. For now, he had more than enough blessings to count and they included this farm, this town, and his family. But the list started and ended with Emma, a woman he would have traded a career to have in his life.

The End

Want more? Check out Calvin and Josie's story in *The Perfect Catch*!

Join Tule Publishing's newsletter for more great reads and weekly deals!

If you enjoyed *Scoring Position*,
you'll love the other books in….

The Texas Playmakers series

Book 1: *The Perfect Catch*

Book 2: *Game On*

Book 3: *Scoring Position*

Available now at your favorite online retailer!

More books by Joanne Rock

The Road to Romance series

Book 1: *Last Chance Christmas*

Book 2: *Second Chance Cowboy*

Book 3: *A Chance This Christmas*

Available now at your favorite online retailer!

About the Author

USA Today bestselling author Joanne Rock writes emotional, sexy romance from fast-paced contemporaries to small-town family sagas. An optimist by nature and perpetual seeker of silver linings, Joanne finds romance fits her life outlook perfectly–love is worth fighting for. When she's not writing, she enjoys long lunches with good friends and walking on the beach as often as possible. A quiet and organized Virgo, Joanne married a fiery and boisterous Aries man in true opposites-attract fashion.